FREYA'S
FRAGRANCE

A romantic novel woven around the story of the
Greeks who wanted to see Jesus

By

Pauline Lewis

'Some Greeks were among those who had gone to Jerusalem to
worship during the festival. They went to Philip and said, 'Sir, we
want to see Jesus.' John 12:20, 21

British Library Cataloguing in Publication Data.
A catalogue record for this book is available from the British Library

978 0 86071 842 0

A Commissioned Publication Printed by

MOORLEYS
Print, Design & Publishing
info@moorleys.co.uk • www.moorleys.co.uk

Foreword

As I read my Bible I love to imagine the lives of those unnamed women whose presence in the stories we may have taken for granted.

I have written two books, Towards the Sunrise, about some of these unnamed women. Noah's wife, a woman who danced with Miriam on the seashore, the importunate widow, and the one who put her last coins into the treasury – all special characters from well- known Bible stories, yet unnamed. I am still on the look-out for further characters to complete book three, but the wife of the nearer kinsman who was unwilling to marry Ruth turned out to be a whole book, The Dark Stranger, and still they come as God shines light on these old familiar stories.

My imagination lighted on the party of Greeks who had asked Philip to arrange for them to meet with Jesus. Who were they? How did they happen to be in Jerusalem at that time? This was the time, not just when Jews gathered to remember the first Passover, but when the true Passover was enacted out by the Saviour, God's own Son, and Jesus died that terrible death so that God's judgement might pass over us.

What might have been the reaction of these Greeks when Philip had to return, embarrassed to explain that Jesus had not agreed to meet with them?

But now, an all important question for me: might there have been any women among these travellers?

By chance I heard a true story, of a child rescued from a shipwreck. They had found her wrapped in a blanket of seaweed, kept alive by air trapped within the weed; the sole survivor from a shipwreck of the boat people. A modern day miracle?

Then why not a child rescued by some spice traders in those days of long ago, and kept with them because of some strange gifting that she had, an awareness of perfume and fragrance?

This, intertwined with yet another modern day miracle of how my friend was made aware of God's presence to heal through a most beautiful perfume that filled her room.

As I thought of writing this story, I realised how much research I would need to do concerning the spices and fragrances which might be interwoven into the story. I decided it would involve too much research. Then I had a word which I believed to be from God; 'Get on and write the book,' with the assurance that the research could come later

And so I began to write, not sure how it would all turn out except with a deep assurance that this Jesus who had refused to meet with those Greeks, had understood that, in the right way and at the right time he would eventually make himself known to them.

As, in obedience, I began to write I found a beautiful story unfolding. I pray that as you read this story of Freya, the Spice Maiden, that you too will share the fragrance of the Saviour, who may also have been called the Rose of Sharon and the Lily of the Valley.

Introduction

In the early days of the Roman Empire, but when it had already become great enough for people to begin to work out their dates by the years of the reigning Caesar, it was rumoured abroad that in the eastern seas were some islands where new and exotic spices had been found growing in abundance. Maybe it was from that time that they had been named the Spice Islands. Who could say? We only know that these soon popular spices had appeared for sale in the markets of China, and even spreading further abroad. Rome had been forcing, not Latin, but strangely Greek as the trade language. They were demanding and overseeing the building of roads – leading to Rome of course, but also sending out war ships to patrol the seas, thus reducing the risk of encounters with pirates. Yes, even in those days of long ago, they were a terrible scourge to trading vessels. Hence the life of spice traders had become less risky.

But there was one thing that even the mighty Roman Empire could not control, and even today with all the wonders of weather forecasting, and that was the weather.

So it was, that this band of Spice Traders, led by one Antonio Castor, having travelled extensively through the markets and lands of Asia Minor and following the silk route into Candalay, at a great price, and in hope of an even greater return of wealth, set out, though with uncertain directions towards these spice islands.

'Land ahead!' The cry from the boy looking out from the rigging, was followed by other cries, not equally welcome.

'O Captain! Look at that cloud formation. Surely that gives warning of a hurricane approaching?'

But as the sailors clustered to the look out, there were cries of horror as pieces of spar and tattered rigging floated past them as the turbulent breakers were now tossing their own ship towards the shore. Captain and crew alike had one purpose now, to row their own ancient vessel into a quiet haven.

Wanting to give thanks to whatever gods many of them served, aghast at the thought of the vessel that had not been fortunate enough to catch but the tail end of the hurricane, old Antonio still had a mind to fortune.

'Captain. My men would like to take the boat to search for any survivors.'

'The captain gave a cursory consent, getting his sailors to work on damage to his own vessel.'

They paddled gently out of the cove where they had taken shelter. 'You'll not find any yet alive, Aba,' one volunteered.

'Maybe not, but I saw two bodies floating past lashed to the mast. They looked to me to have some vestments and jewellery that might be worth a lot.'

Even as they talked the men were dragging some corpses to the side, searching and then discarding them to the mercy of the waves.

'Hey! Here we are!' As they pulled into a further cove Antonio spied the bodies he had seen earlier.

'Now! Now lads! Just leave this to your Aba! I'll see you get your share. Deftly he slipped something from the neck of the woman who was still clasped tightly in the arms of the man, while he in turn remained lashed firmly to the mast of the vessel which had kept their bodies afloat.

'Rich man,' Antonio observed. 'Obviously he must be the one who chartered the ship.' He pulled his beard. 'Don't know what gods he prayed to, but he could not have done enough to command their protection. He fingered the silver locket that he had taken from the dead and cautiously slipped it into the leather pouch he wore around his neck.

They had returned to the bay and pulled the small boat onto the shingle when Jona, one of his men, shouted out and dashed back into the foaming surf. 'Look Aba, look.'

'Why are you bothering? It's just a blanket of seaweed.'

'No! No! There is something alive.' He picked up the slimy bundle and dragged it onto the sand. As he probed in the mass, the rest of the men, curious, gathered around. There was a choking cry, a gurgle, and there, looking up into the watching faces, a child – yes, a little girl, gulping and choking, then letting out a lusty scream - yes, a child who was very definitely alive.

PART 1 - SPICE MAIDEN
CHAPTER 1
MIRACLE CHILD

The storms were long past and Antonio and his group of spice merchants were sitting in the bow of the ship they had hired as it made speed back to the mainland. It was for the sake of the rescued child as much as anything, for the spice merchants could well have spent longer collecting these precious spicy nuts that had so recently been discovered.

The men nudged each other, looking toward the captain. He was not speaking in the pigeon Greek, the trade language by which they all managed to communicate, but though they could not understand his words, they were well aware that he was not happy. Guessing what the problem was, Antonio stood up and lurched his way below. It was as he had guessed. There was the missing cabin boy, a contented little girl sitting on his knee while he fed her. Yes, it was his own ration of dry biscuit, but mashed up into a soggy mess with goat's milk, but it staved off her hunger.

'Better get back up to the captain, lad,' Antonio advised, 'or he will be throwing the baby back into the sea, and you with her.' Aba, as his own men called him, was happy enough to have his turn to hold the frail little girl, while she seemed content to have her choice of nurse maids.

When they had first found this miracle child who had survived the ship wreck, wrapped up in a blanket of seaweed, it hadn't seemed possible that she could survive. Her limbs hung lifeless, while, without strength to cry, she could only let out a thin whine.

The islanders who had run to the shore, grasping the situation, had soon returned with a young woman, her breasts full enough to feed her own as well as this little orphan, and when the ship was ready to sail, there they were with a nanny goat and her kid as a ready supply of milk for their journey.

Freya! It was one of the sailors who had named her. Evidently he had had a little sister of that name who, sadly, had died, but the name had stuck, so Freya she was. The cabin boy had woven a little harness of rope, and they had to make sure that she was always secured if one or other of them were not holding her, for surely she had had enough adventures to last a life time.

But the captain was still muttering threats and when he mentioned that they were expecting to call in at a port shortly on the mainland Aba had a dread that he might be thinking of selling the child.

Doubtless it was not any feelings of sentimentality that made the old man determined to protect the child from such traffic. Perhaps he was concerned for the profit he himself might make, for he held something precious in his leather pouch which always hung around his neck. He turned seaward now, so that others were not aware, but he reached in to finger it. Yes, it was the precious silver locket which he had snatched from the neck of Freya's mother.

Antonio and his group of Spice Traders left the ship when they had arrived back on the mainland, and though there were sad farewells from many of the crew, and yes, tears from the cabin boy, he had made sure that the little toddler, Freya was among them.

As they made their way westward there were many offers to feed the child, and to take her to hearts and homes, but Aba would have none of that. Though his motives might have been dubious, he was determined that he had a vested interest in the child and she should not be snatched from them.

Freya had been happy as she was seated on the shoulders of one or another of the traders, but she changed from a curious toddler back to a fretful baby, letting out her thin whine once she again saw a harbour with its array of ships and smaller boats. But his men were footsore and weary, for they had travelled overland many miles to come within reach of the Great Sea, and of all the options, to take ship again was their safest way of reaching home. But would this ensure a home for their miracle child?

She settled down again once they had set sail, and having landed safely back on the mainland of Greece each had set out for his own home.

'Come, my little Freya. We will find a home for you, where you will be loved and cared for. You will be safe, your Aba will see to that.' He tried to sound confident, but could he be sure that his wife Yasha would give the child a welcome?

CHAPTER 2
A HOME FOR FREYA

Maria was standing on the hill that stood guard over the old family farm. Only two of the fields had been ploughed and planted this year, for her sons had left home and grudgingly returned to the old homestead from time to time to help their mother. It was enough for her to care for the chickens and her few goats.

She liked to climb the hill and look out on the bustling scenes of life in the port below them. It was good to be reminded that there was more to life than the dwindling presence of her own family. Dwindling for her, of course, but for her one son and two daughters, all recently married, it was only just beginning. They all promised they would come and visit, but she could see it was more likely it was she who would have to visit them.

Maria had squatted down on a hummock, but rose now as she thought she recognised some men who were waiting on the quayside as their bundles were being thrown to them from the hold of the little fishing vessel. Someone turned away from settling his account with the captain. Yes, she had thought he had looked familiar. Could it be that old curmudgeon Antonio?

There was a time when he could have set her heart beating, yes, even after he had married his beautiful Yasha and they had a cottage full of children, but she had learned to be older and wiser, and though she still missed her husband, Simon, codger though she had often called him, she didn't know what it was she was longing for to fill the deep loneliness in her life.

She had turned to go into her cottage and stirred up her fire. She had a feeling Antonio was making his way to her door and she did not want to appear too welcoming. Emerging from the darkness of her home she sat in the sunshine on the bench that enabled her to lean against the warmed stones of her cottage.

With a start she awoke, for it was so easy to drift into slumber with the murmur of the bees, and the fragrance of the lavender she had planted near her door. Yes, sure enough, the old trader was making his way up the pathway, his sack a heavy load on his shoulder, but there was a lad with him, and he had a different burden. Could it be she had heard the piping voice of a little child? Was it this had awakened her? Yes, her eyes were not deceiving her, for a child sat confidently astride the shoulders of the boy and now Aba

3

was reaching up to take her, and carried her to place the little girl in Maria's lap.

The child snuggled confidently into Maria's ample bosom. 'Mamma, Mamma' she murmured.

Aba had seated himself beside them. 'Well!' was the only word that came to his lips. 'Well! I knew I was meant to bring her to you, but I didn't dare to hope for such a reaction.'

'Or such a reaction from me, either, I dare say?' Maria chuckled, 'for I was determined not to let you wheedle your way into my life again, whatever your plan this time.......' She turned to give instructions to the lad who had been carrying Freya to take a mug from the house and go and milk the goat so the child could drink and then it wasn't long before they had stirred up the fire and the pot of stew which had been readied on the fire was satisfying them all. Freya had slipped from her Nona's lap, as Aba had decreed Maria should be called, and happily sat on the grass with her own dish and spoon. She had learned many a skill since she had been rescued, all those long months before.

Their dishes refilled until everyone's hunger was eased, Freya slipped back onto Maria's lap and slept while Aba, with the lad putting in his own version now and again, told the story of the miracle that had brought this little bundle of life eventually to her door.

'But it seems like another miracle that Freya took to you straight away and called you Mamma too. I was determined not to let her be sold for filthy lucre as they say, and I didn't know how my own wifey was going to react.'

Antonio took out a handful of nuts from his pocket and sat contentedly chewing while Maria, thinking she had better not let him get too comfy, began to busy herself making up a little bed for her Freya. Having eventually waved them off, it was when Maria took the balls of myrrh which she had slipped inside her clothes at the approach of visitors and was about to return to the clay jar where she stored them that again she noted Freya's reaction.

'Mamma, Mamma,' she murmured contentedly, lifting up her arms to her adopted grandmother.

Hm, hmm. Maria stored that memory in her heart. She too felt a deep contentment. But was there a bonding here which could last?

CHAPTER 3
MYRRH

Antonio could hear the crying of the gulls, swooping after the fishing vessels coming into the harbour way below, but he was more aware of the flock of children who had been playing among the olive groves. There seemed to be one who had become their accepted leader. Her limbs were not of the olive brown of the other children, but she was fair of skin and instead of their shiny black tresses her hair was a mop of gold.

Antonio could scarcely recognise the little life they had rescued from the ship wreck, - though it had seemed as if the seaweed had been sent to rescue her before they had come along; but there was no doubt that it was she, for she had left her playmates and confidently run up to the old Spice Trader and placing her hand in his, led him along the path to Maria's cottage, chatting happily all the way.

But Maria did not give him so warm a welcome. Arms akimbo she barred his way into the cottage, though Freya had already dived past her into the dim interior to stir up the fire and see that the pot of stew was soon bubbling.

'And what do you think you are doing here, you old rogue?' challenged Maria, for two winters had passed since he had left Freya with Maria, but Aba as they knew him, was not to be put off.

'Now don't you worry,' he laughed. 'I can see you are doing a wonderful job, but don't forget she is my treasure too, and I have to keep an eye on my vested interests.'

Without being invited he had seated himself on the bench beside the door, leaning back and searching in his pocket for his ubiquitous nuts. Patting the seat for Maria to sit beside him he asked, 'Tell me, does she still call you Mamma?'

'Oh, goodness me no,' she responded. 'I could not allow that. What would people think? No, I am her Nona, her grandmother.'

They sat quietly for a while, happy to watch the child bustling capably about. Then Maria turned the conversation back to when he had first arrived with the child and her murmur of 'Mamma.'

'I puzzled over that, you know,' Maria told him. 'I didn't hear her say that again until we were at the market place, and very occasionally she would sit

5

quietly beside someone and quietly question, 'Mamma?' Then one day there was a woman who was selling myrrh. I could not get Freya to leave her. I realised that somehow she was linking myrrh with her mother.'

'But you? Were you wearing myrrh?'

If her skin were not so toughened and wrinkled you might have detected a blush rising up from her neck. But Maria laughed. 'O aye, I keep some in a little jar and tuck it in my bosom to give me confidence if I am in an unknown situation.'

Aba gave her a gentle dig in her ribs, 'or maybe some old flame on the horizon?'

Maria pushed him away indignantly, but as they began to enjoy the stew little Freya had served them, she added 'Well, it certainly helped me to bond with my little one.'

CHAPTER 4
SPICE MAIDEN IN DEMAND

Freya and her foster grandmother Maria had been happily tending their little patch of garden when Freya suddenly laid aside her trowel and hurried into the cottage.

Maria looked up, amazed, for though the girl's quick hearing had heard them approaching, it was a few moments before she caught sight of their visitors.

While Freya had already stirred up the fire so that soon enough their inevitable stew pot was bubbling on the grate, Maria stood, defensively, to greet Antonio. The lad with him hung back by the gate, realising they might not be made welcome.

'Now then, what sort of welcome is this?' old Antonio chided, while Maria, taking hold of his even bushier beard, shook it.

'Three harvests have passed since we have had sight or sound of you and you come expecting to snatch my treasure away from me.'

'Oh come, my beautiful Maria,' he coaxed, trying to slip his arm around her and coax her to relax into a more welcoming frame of mind. 'I left my most treasured investment in your care. You would not drive me away now, would you, for I have a great request to make of you?'

Freya emerged from the house, her head scarf tied neatly and wearing a clean pinafore. She sought to coax the two to be seated amicably but Antonio's attention was turned now from the ripe beauty of Maria to the delicate flower that was fast emerging from the cocoon that they had found wrapped up and so miraculously preserved in the blanket of seaweed, so long ago now.

'Treasure indeed,' he continued, as, ignoring his evident admiration, Freya continued to set the stools and carry out a platter of bread, cheese, olives and grapes, soon followed with bowls of the familiar stew. She was aware of the lad hanging about at the gate and nodded to him to join them.

It wasn't until the bowls were empty, and he had wiped his bushy beard dry with the cloths their little maid had supplied that Antonio, happy now to hear them call him by the familiar 'Aba' felt he dare speak of his mission. What a difference does a full stomach make.

He turned to Maria. 'You have always had a reputation as a good cook,' he began, 'but when last I visited you I realised that there were herbs and spices added to the stew which gave it a yet more special zing.'

Maria wanted to defend her own cooking skills, but Aba was continuing. 'Now now Maria, no one can deny your skills, but nor can you deny that our Freya has gifts of her own, for this time again I recognise yet new flavours. Come, I am not a spice trader of repute for nothing.

'Why, look in your garden. I see herbs here growing that were never here before.'

Maria sat quietly, while Freya, having cleared the dishes had slipped into the garden, nodding to the lad to join her, gathered a few herbs from here and there and placed them quietly beside Antonio. Amazed, he lifted them to his nose.

'I can't deny it.' Maria at last began to speak.

'Do you remember how she always responded to the fragrance of myrrh? I couldn't get over it that she had immediately called me Mamma, but then, when the same thing happened as we mingled amongst the women at the market, I began to wonder. I remembered how she would run up and seek to clamber into the lap of certain women.

'Then, at last I learned that if ever she seemed unsettled or fearful I would slip a bundle of myrrh into my bosom and immediately she would snuggled up to me and sometimes murmur, 'Mamma?' I realised at last that the myrrh was awakening some memory.'

Unwillingly, it seemed, Antonio had to admit, yes, there had been a bundle of myrrh around the corpse of her mother.

But how could it have survived the ship wreck? Maria did not ask, but Antonio could see the question in her eyes. Almost grudgingly, it seemed, he admitted that it had been in a special locket which she had hung around her neck.

'And you are not going to show us, are you?' Maria was challenging, but they were both making sure they kept their voices low, for the child was still in the house.

'Think, woman,' he hissed. 'It is my responsibility to guard it for her. It is not a plaything for a child. Surely you can understand that. But she has other treasure that we must guard, for if we can find out the names of these herbs and spices, then we can begin to cultivate them, store their seeds and eventually begin to trade with them.

'I'll return in a few days and we'll go to the market and see what we discover.' And brooking no argument from the doughty Maria, he called a farewell to Freya. Briefly he told her of their plans. She happily responded to his grandfatherly hug and remained at the gate waving her farewell as he toiled back up the path. But then, suddenly, she begged him to wait as she turned to her garden and gathering a little posy of the sweet saxifrage, ran back to her Aba to tell him it was for him to take back to his wife.

Had the child an understanding that he had plans which would mean him once again leaving his wife and family?

CHAPTER 5
CALL FROM THE NORTH

A sudden snap in the weather had covered the hillsides and the little cottage garden with a sprinkling of snow. Maria awakened to search out a long forgotten blanket and with it wrapped around her had run to stir up the embers of the fire. Once it was blazing she put on a special log she had stored for such a rare emergency.

'Don't you worry, my little one. I'll soon have a mug of hot ginger to warm the cockles of your heart,' she chatted away, but when there was no response she ran to the inner room so see if Freya had refused to leave her bed. Eventually she realised the door was not made fast.

'Freya?' she called from the doorway, loathe to leave the fire, and was amazed to find the child in the garden, thrilled not only to see the snow, but she was gathering it in her hands and throwing it into the air.

'Oh Nona! Nona! What is it? It is so beautiful. I have never seen it before.'

'No indeed. It does not belong here. This is what they have in those northern lands. I know we get plenty of rain in the winter, but my bones are not made to welcome Jack Frost. You had better come and help me get a pot of stew ready, with all our hottest spices to warm us up.'

But she could not keep her Spice Maiden inside for long until eventually she came running to the cottage to tell her that Aba was on his way. And he did not need to be told to take the seat nearest to the fire, where he held out his hands to the warming mug of spiced tea that Maria had soon prepared for him.

'Is there no fire in your house that you have come scrounging round to us to be warmed?'

Shameless, Antonio laughed. 'Couldn't get near our fire for little ones,' he told her. 'They are not like our Freya. I found her out on the hills, having the time of her life.'

'But where has it come from?' Maria tried to push his chair over so that she could draw hers nearer to the blaze. 'I was telling the lassie that this is weather that comes from the northern lands, and does not belong on our sunny shores.'

Antonio sat quietly, rubbing his beard. 'I wonder,' he said. 'I wonder.'

'Wonder what?' Maria asked when he relapsed into silence.

'Well – look at her! Her parents could not have been from around here. She is different from the local children, - her hair, her skin, her eyes. And see her reaction to the snow.'

'I have told her that this weather is what they have in the northern lands – though not sure how I know that. I haven't travelled far. Not like you, Aba.'

The two sat quietly, pondering and then light seemed to dawn on them both.

'Her parents! We don't know where they came from. It could well be.'

Freya came in at that moment and held out her poor little frozen hands for Maria to gently warm, then she too was on a little stool by the fire, a fresh mug of ginger in her hands.

'Talking about northern lands,' Antonio volunteered after a quiet pause –

'Yes?' asked Maria, while Freya looked at them both expectantly.

The old man fingered his beard, and coughed nervously.

'No need to be nervous,' Maria laughed. 'We know you are bound to be on your travels again. I don't know what has kept you at home these past, is it three years now? So where are you off to this time?'

'O, tell us, tell us Aba!' Freya was on her feet, dancing around him expectantly, though there was little enough space in Maria's cottage.

'Sit down, girl, for goodness sake,' Maria scolded. 'And I don't know why you are getting so excited, child, for it is the men who are going, not you.'

Antonio found his voice now. 'But that's just it, Maria. I need our little spice maiden to come with us …..

'Now now,' he continued, for Maria had jumped to her feet as if about to fetch her wooden stirring spoon with which to clobber him.

'No, I wouldn't take the child away from her Nona. ' Maria felt she could breathe again, but then he continued,

'Nor would I think of going on this journey without our Freya, for she has a wonderful gift of recognising fragrances and herbs.'

Freya took over the task of adding herbs now and extra vegetables to the ubiquitous pot that was always on the fire, for she could see that there was going to be a long discussion.

After arguing about all the logistics of a long journey, as well as the risk of having women travelling with their party, let alone a beautiful young girl, at last Maria got round to her fear of shipwrecks if they travelled overseas.

'No, no,' Aba promised. 'We'll be steering away from the usual trade routes this time and heading north, for I'm hearing rumours of untold riches in a land called Persia.

'And I'm encouraging some of the younger men to bring their wives along, and that will discourage them from attracting followers, and anger from the locals.'

Warmed thoroughly, and confident that he would get his way, he left his greatest treasure in the care of Maria, promising to return to the little cottage in the Spring.

Meanwhile, once the weather had resumed its usual milder temperature, accompanied by an inevitable abundance of rain, Freya was dragging her Maria, complaining maybe, to the market. She continued her search for strange herbs and spices, but most of all she was enquiring for news of this strange Northern land of Persia, and especially the fragrant frankincense Antonio had mentioned.

Then one day a woman was there with some yellow powder which she told them could be used to make some biscuit-like cakes. Maria turned up her nose at the strange flavour, but it wasn't long before she had been persuaded to purchase this new spice and they were off home to see what they could do. Most of all Freya was so excited to hear that this special hitherto unknown spice had come from the land of Persia. Oh, surely, surely they would be on their way soon. But little did she know what far greater treasure she was soon to encounter.

CHAPTER 6
THE JOURNEY BEGINS

Maria had done her best to persuade the old man to wait a year or two, and circumstances in his family conspired so that their Freya would soon be approaching adolescence when at last the message came. They were to join the team of traders who were gathering in the town and once they were all assembled they would be off.

Poor Maria. There was so much to think of. They had walked over the hill to where one of her sons had a small holding, and bartered with him for the loan of one of his donkeys in order to carry their loads, for they would need a tent of goat skin for when they slept in the open air. Goat skin water bottles too, and of course hard rations as we might call them, all had to be stored securely for the long journey.

It was when Andros, the carpenter came to board up the cottage that Freya realised that this great adventure was more than just a dream, but that indeed they were on their way.

Oh, what arguing and bartering and shouting was going on, and of course the local people were taking advantage of the excitement and persuading them to eat the food they had been preparing for them before at last they set off.

The first day or two the men, yes and the few women who had been pressed into accompanying them, were in familiar territory, but for Freya it was all new and exciting.

Maria tried to advise her to conserve her energy for the many miles, and mountains too, that yet lay between them and the strange land of Persia they were seeking, and that it was no good her trying to gather the plants they found on their way, for they could not take fresh treasure on board before they had sold some of the goods they were carrying.

Maria was a hardy village woman, used to walking many a long mile or labouring in the fields for many a long hour, yet she and some of the other women were beginning to complain, while Freya seemed to have an insatiable appetite to explore the unknown. Yet she was tender hearted and concerned for her dear Nona, and understood that she did not have the same incentive to face hardship.

'Aba,' she whispered to old Antonio, who was always in the lead. 'Don't you worry, my lass', he reassured her. 'Those travellers we passed yesterday said that it is only a few hours before we reach a prosperous town. We'll find a safe place to set up our tents, and settle there for a few days. You wait until the women see the wonderful garments that are for sale, the jewellery and other wonders that they will have and they will forget all about their sore feet and being home sick. Oh yes, and healing balms and things to enhance their beauty. When you grow up you will understand that it isn't just food for their stomachs that women need, but food for their eyes and to satisfy their pride too.'

Freya ran back to give her version of the old man's forecast, while Antonio began to make his own preparation.

Once they were gathered to settle for the night he gave them all strict instruction of the caution they needed to take once they were in the town. But little did he know of what adventures lay ahead of them.

CHAPTER 7
HARVEST OF GOLD

As Antonio had predicted, Maria and her friends had found delight in the market place and some of the comforts of that strange Macedonian township, and they sat around the little fires they had lit and stirred their delicious meals, thus trading their food for some of the other delights that were for sale.

Meanwhile Freya was flitting to and fro, watching what the local women used in their cooking and running back with samples for Maria to try. Antonio would check up with the girl every now and again, for he was on the lookout for this strange yellow powder, saffron as we would know it, but names would change from place to place, so who knew what they might have called it.

They had moved on, with much moaning and complaining from Freya's beloved Maria, but the girl understood that it was hard for the older woman and knew that it was for her sake that she had agreed to come, so she ran back often to encourage her, and give her a hug to assure her of her appreciation.

At last they had reached the little known kingdom of Persia, with its strange temples, and clothes and languages too. Freya was always ready to greet people, and especially among the young, but they often met blank stares, for though Greek was supposed to be the universal language there were not many who understood or spoke it. They were rarely in need of directions though, for well-worn foot-paths had soon become high ways.

Very occasionally there would be a shout and they had to dismount their donkeys and drag the unwilling beasts to the side of the road, even flinging themselves into a ditch while men on horseback galloped, or if the hill was steep, plodded past them.

Freya had on one very rare occasion seen some Roman soldiers in their home town but they did not look as fierce as these ones.

'No, no. These are Persians,' Antonio informed her. 'And make sure they do not notice you. I do not want pretty little girls getting us into trouble.'

'I thought I was supposed to look like a boy?' Freya queried, for her guardians had decided that that might be for her safety.

'Oh aye. We've done our best, but you'd better get Maria to cut your hair again.'

It was while they had set up camp in one of the northern towns and Freya was happily wandering from stall to stall, or should I say, from cooking pot to cooking pot, that she suddenly broke away from the lads who had been told to always keep their eye on her.

'Aba! Aba!' she gasped. Antonio was deep into some negotiation with one of the locals when this lad, as they were supposed to think, came pulling at his sleeve, demanding attention.

Eventually, having come to some arrangement with the dealer, he turned to her.

'Tuck your hair in,' he growled. 'What is it? It had better be important.'

'The yellow powder, Aba. There is a woman who has some. She is making little cakes.'

'Show me! Show me!' His displeasure was forgotten. Oh yes, this was important enough. She led him swiftly through the many little stalls and groups of people.

'There Aba.' Antonio knew he could trust Freya's judgement. She would not lead him astray. Could this be the saffron they were seeking? And if it was, could it be for sale, something he could buy in bulk?

*   *   *   *

Maria had been complaining about the shaking of the old ox cart that Antonio had hired to carry them up into the hills, but eventually she was lulled by the patient plod of the beasts and was nodding off to sleep.

But not her Freya! Oh no. Life was one long adventure for her. Sometimes she and the lads would clamber down and run along- side the cart, sometimes lagging behind as they followed a little stream, or sought to make conversation with one of the local peasants. But their Aba always had his eye on them and they were all aboard when first a murmur, and then an excited shout rose up, for away in the distance, what a sight met their eyes.

'Gold! Gold!' they were exclaiming. The patient oxen plodded on until at last they were near enough to see the over-all effect of gold was made up of thousand upon thousand of the beautiful little crocus flowers, their stamen sprouted out, waiting to be gathered for this lucrative spice trade.

Antonio and the older men were soon sitting round with the owners of the field, while they all were made welcome with various juices and stronger drink and the traditional cheeses with the small flat loaves which seemed to be a basic for hospitality.

Freya, of course, was deeply interested and aware of all that was going on and they all clapped with glee when at last some small sacks of the precious spice were safely loaded onto their cart.

'Right, off we go,' Aba called to the drivers. 'We must make haste to make sure we are back into the town before night fall.' Maria's eyes were already closed, and Antonio too soon beginning to nod, but not Freya. She, with the resilience of youth, would sleep deep and sound every night but not in the day light. Every moment was to be savoured, each new day a wonderful gift.

Antonio was alert now, for he had heard Freya's name and he became aware that the young ones were no longer following their cart.

'Freya!' His voice bellowed out, but there was no response from the girl. Mika, one of Maria's grandsons, supposed to keep special watch over her, gesticulated helplessly, and soon most of them were out of the cart and had gathered about her.

Maria tried to put her arms around her special child but Freya shrugged her off. Antonio raised his arm as if he wanted to strike her but Maria quickly intervened. But what was the matter with the girl?

There were tears in her eyes, and yet a strange light on her face as if of rapturous joy.

Maria tried a very gentle shake. 'Freya, my love. What is it? Tell us, for Aba is anxious we get back to the town before night falls. Why have you stopped here?'

Freya turned her big eyes upon them. 'Can't you smell it?' Shaking heads was all the response they gave her. 'Oh, it is the most wonderful perfume. I have never ever been aware of anything so beautiful.' ……

She pulled away from them a little and climbed up the bank beside the road. There, in the far distance among the trees was a strangely shaped building with a dome. Freya turned to appeal to their Aba.

Antonio was learning never to ignore the impressions of this child.

'Freya,' he pleaded. 'I promise I will bring you back, but we must get back to the town before night fall or we may not be even alive by morning.' Gently they coaxed her back into the cart but she seemed to be in a daze.

CHAPTER 8
FREYA'S FRAGRANCE

Freya tossed and turned that night, and when she did at last fall into a restless sleep it was to dream of a treasure chest. It was entwined in chains of seaweed and when eventually they had managed to drag in onto dry land they were still struggling to open it.

She awoke to find it was daylight and Maria already cooking some breakfast. 'Oh Maria, I'm sorry. Why didn't you wake me? Oh, how soon are we setting off?'

'Come here my love and see how much there is to be seen.'

Grabbing her robe, she joined her Nona to peer outside, but quickly closed the flap and huddled by the fire. Maria took her pot off the hob and gave herself to comforting her child, who was quietly shuddering with sobs.

'He promised, Nona, he promised,' was all she kept repeating.

'Yes, yes, and he will keep his promise as soon as it is possible. But we can't travel in this heavy mist. Come, help me to make this pottage and we'll all feel better, and who knows what will turn up.'

Something, or rather someone did turn up, for out of the mist had come a young lad, who obviously had a story to tell. The mist was lifting and Antonio had invited him to his tent. They were sitting drinking a mint tea when Freya joined them. She had a look about her as if she were still in a dream, even as she gazed into the face of the youth.

An older man had already appeared, offering to help to interpret so that they could communicate. But before a word had passed, Freya's face was alight. 'The fragrance,' she whispered to Maria. 'Very very faint, but it is the same.' Had it come from his garments, or somehow from the boy himself?

In spite of the inclement weather and her great disappointment, the morning passed happily as eventually they sorted out the message the youth had come to bring to them.

The fragrance? It seemed that his own father was a servant who worked for the Wise Man, as he was called, living in the strange building they had spotted so high up in the hills: high up to be nearer to the sky it seemed, for the roundel on the roof of his house was where he went to study the stars.

It seems that someone had run to the big house and told the master of these foreigners who were planning to return, and it was he who had sent them this envoy.

It was the boy's own father who was one of the servants who had accompanied the master on a very great adventure. The Master, old now to think of making the journey into the town, would like to meet this youth, as he thought. Maybe, just maybe he might have the strength to tell this young person who had been so aware of the heavenly fragrance what he remembered of that amazing journey.

That night Freya's sleep was undisturbed. She did dream, just before the sun crept through the slit of their tent, and again it was of the box of treasure, but now she awoke confident that it would yield to their efforts to open it.

She heard the clip clop of donkeys as they clattered over a rocky pavement at the entrance to the field where they had been permitted to set up their camp, and the young girl who had been assigned to bring fresh water for the women as well as to remove their waste had already done her duties, but the servant girl had seemed to be almost as excited as Freya, who by now seemed to be bubbling over with joy.

Because of the camping arrangements at least, it was evident that Freya was no boy, but still they dressed her in the garments of a youth.

Antonio had been aware of the interest of a rich young merchant in their beautiful Freya and had not been surprised when he had approached him offering rich gifts in return for marriage. Aba had insisted she was much too young for such an arrangement, and warned Maria and others of their party to keep her out of sight, but it was not so much to do with her age, but of her great value to him in their spice trade that made him so anxious to protect her.

Meanwhile Freya was already fed and, mounted on one of the donkeys, and with the party sent to accompany her, was trotting along the mountain road drinking in the story that her escort was telling her. She was supposed to be accompanying him so that she could hear this special story from the lips of the boy's father. But it seemed he could not wait until they reached their destination and now there seemed to be a double miracle, for not only were these two young people communicating without trouble, but Jasper, as she learned he was named, was telling the story as fluently as he had heard it so many times from his father.

'Our Master, the Wise One as everyone called him, was enthralled with fragrance, but also with the stories of the stars. He had this observatory built and my father and the other servants would help him to roll back the covers so that he could study the journey of the stars through the heavens. He had these old manuscripts too and was obsessed with these studies. Often he would forget to eat, and would never sleep if the night was clear.

'Then at last he was sure that he had seen a new star. He was convinced that it was a special message from the Creator to tell him that a child was born, the one promised from long ago in the Hebrew Scriptures.

'From then on there was no rest for any of us. Messengers were sent to those other Wise Ones who shared his interest in the Holy Books as well as the stars, and they returned with the news that they too had prepared gifts and were already setting out.'

Freya could hardly believe that they had already reached the spot where she had first caught sight of the strange building with its roof open to the heavens, and yes, where she had become aware of the fragrance.

They clambered down from the donkeys. Freya didn't see who it was who had come to lead them away, for she only had eyes for what was yet to be unfolded. A door opened as they reached the building and hands reached out to give them refreshing drinks, but then she heard a gasp from Jasper who had been escorting her for, from an inner sanctum he had seen his own father, yes, but he was beckoning Freya to enter to meet another. She heard him whisper, 'It is the Wise One.'

CHAPTER 9
THE WISE ONE

Freya forgot about her aching limbs as soon as she had slipped from her donkey and heard the clip clop as the beasts were led away. Who now would interpret for her? But from Jasper's reaction she was aware that it was the Wise One himself who was climbing steadily before her up the winding stair case until at last they reached the chamber of the stars, as she thought of it.

'Oh, my!' She stood gazing in wonder at the glory of the heavens, though eventually she realised that the roof was still closed and the stars and planets she saw had been painted onto the ceiling.

'Sit, my daughter.' The sound she heard came through the growth of a beard of many years, yet it did not seem to be the voice of an old man, and again she was not aware of any difficulty in understanding him.

When Antonio, and Maria too, had questioned her about this, she said she thought he had been speaking Greek, though they had only ever used the local dialect in their own village. And no, it certainly had not been in the trade lingo. She had not had time to ponder about this at the time, for she had sat in silent amazement at the story that was pouring from the old man's bearded lips.

'My father before me was a Wise One. He taught me to read many languages and had gathered many holy books and manuscripts. He taught me to read the wonders written in the heavens and to understand the messages of the stars.

'He brought scholars to teach me the wonders of the herbs of the fields and the treasures of the mines and like you, I was very aware of the various fragrances. It was long ago that a trader from Africa brought to me samples of this wonderful aromatic gum resin from a tree that grew there and I knew that this was a treasure fit for a king ………………..'

He paused, seemingly overcome with emotion, as he recalled the way he had been led, and Freya hardly dare breathe lest he was unable to continue. She was longing to ask about this aromatic gum, but knew that had to wait.

'When at last I saw this new star, I knew it was bringing us the message that the king we had read of in the ancient Hebrew scriptures, one who would bring us salvation was coming in this our day. So I sent messages to my colleagues, these other Wise Ones, and suggested that we prepare gifts worthy to bring to this Holy One.'

'And you..?' Freya began to interrupt. She wanted to ask about this very special fragrance – could it be the same as that of which she had been made aware as they had been returning from the fields of saffron, but the Wise Man raised his finger to his lips and she knew she must trust him, and continue to listen.

'Frankincense,' he told her, as if reading her thought. 'Yes, I sent traders all over our known world to get the very best, and I had it stored in a jewelled casket of great wonder. But it is only since I gave this great treasure as my gift to the King that it is as if he has given it back to me as a lingering fragrance.

'It was when the lad Jasper told his father, and he in turn told me of your awareness of the fragrance that I knew I must make a way for you to hear my story.'

A servant slipped in, but the Wise One was not happy at the interruption.

'They are reminding me that you have a long journey to make before nightfall, but this story is far more important.'

Hunger pains and other bodily functions came to disturb but were forgotten as Freya continued to listen enthralled, following with the Wise Men who, all those years ago had joined him in his tower. When they too had seen the star shining so brightly, this previously unseen star that was telling them of the birth of the King of all kings, together they had set out on their long and dangerous journey. In her imagination Freya travelled with them as each night they had checked on the star and knew they must continue to speed on their way.

It seemed that somehow, once they knew they were approaching Jerusalem they had forgotten to do this nightly check and it was the great but false king Herod who had directed them to Bethlehem. Bethlehem? Was that a place for the birth of this heavenly king? The king's own wise men had read to them from their holy book and yes, when they checked with the stars there it was, shining so clearly and so brightly, and directing them still onward – until - yes, it was directly overhead, not over a palace as they had thought, but over a humble little cottage.

'Oh the joy!' The Wise One had risen from his seat and had his arms outstretched again to the heavens, recalling their joy, knowing that, in spite of all the rigors of the journey - disappointments too, they were about to meet the One who was the source and completion of the joy of every living soul and indeed of all creation.

Freya waited in suspense, for he was sat again, silently wiping a tear from his eye. Go on, she had wanted to urge but knew she must not disturb him.

'No, I did not send a servant ahead of us. I took the lead. Gently knocking on the door, I pushed it open – and there he was, the Holy Child. We did not have to ask. We learned after this the story of how he was born, of how he received his name, Jesus; and of how Joseph knew God was calling him to be a father and provider for this King of kings as well as for his mother, Mary.

'Before we thought of unpacking our gifts and presenting them, we prostrated ourselves on the ground in worship.'

Freya felt as if she were there with them and though she dare not move for fear of disturbing this holy atmosphere, in her heart she too was prostrate.

A woman who all this time had been sitting quietly beside her father was taking Freya's hand. Servants had entered silently and were lighting some lamps.

'Don't worry. It is too late for your party to return to the town. We have prepared refreshments for you and a place for you to sleep and you can set out at first light.'

Freya should have been concerned for her dear Maria waiting for her return, but her thoughts were still away in a little home in Bethlehem where she had joined in the joy of the Wise Ones as they knew the star had led them aright, and then, - and then, yes, they had entered in and actually seen the Child, but even more than that, she had joined them in worshipping him, not only King of the Jews, but King of kings.

But what about the fragrance?

CHAPTER 10
TREASURE OF GREAT WORTH

'Oh Maria, I had not been aware that there was any one else in that tower until this beautiful woman stood up and led me safely down the stairs to her room. She gave me food and then let me sleep in a bed beside hers. Then very early in the morning she brought me food for the journey and we came out and found the others in our group ready to bring me safely back to you.'

Freya could not doubt that her Maria was delighted to see her child returned to her safely but what was going on in their camp? Her Nona didn't seem to be very interested in hearing of her adventure. She was bustling about, packing blankets and pots and pans, as well as preparing food for yet another journey.

'What is going on?' she demanded, but Maria continued bustling around her. 'Go and ask your Aba,' she shouted at her. 'We just have to do what we are told.'

Freya snorted, trying to hide her amusement, for she knew well enough that her Maria would not be pushed around by anyone, not even their Aba; but Antonio appeared then and called the girl aside.

'Your Maria was more than willing when I said I thought it was best if we discontinued this journey. Thanks to you we have done some good trading and accumulated wealth that will last us for a while, but if we continue along the Spice Road we will be in danger of robbers for word will have gone ahead that we have with us something of great worth.'

'Have we?' Freya's expression formed her surprise.

'We have indeed.' Antonio stood arms akimbo, and after some moments of silence went on to explain.

Seating himself on one of the packed saddle bags, he gestured for Freya to do the same. Once he had her full attention he continued.

'It is you, our Freya, who is our greatest treasure. I have known it, ever since you were a toddler, and you know that is why you and your Maria have come with us on our travels. But now everyone is aware of it, for word is spreading far and wide that you were called to visit with the Wise One. So many have sought this privilege but he has remained, hidden away, far off from the world.'

'But, but …..?'

'You don't understand how I feel I must hide you away?' Antonio sought to put words into her mouth. At last he felt she was beginning to understand.

'Yes, Freya. Armed robbers might come to seize you, and then demand a king's ransom, or even keep you as a slave to work for them.'

Maria had left her frantic packing and had slipped quietly to join them. Standing behind the girl, her arms were around her, pressing her to her bosom.

'There, there, my Lamb. Don't fear. Aba will see that we are taken safely back to our farm.'

'Come now, let's get things moving, and not a word of our plans to anyone. There is that rich young Greek who is ready to pay me a great price if I will allow him to take her for his bride.'

Maria shook her fist in indignation. 'She is still a child! Such a suggestion!'

'Yes, yes,' agreed Antonio. 'but all the same, we'll leave quietly so that he doesn't know where we are gone. But we'll still try to keep her disguised as a lad, though it didn't work for him too well. And keep those locks of gold tucked inside her cap, or someone will think her of great worth for her hair alone.'

Maria sighed as she returned to her task. Would they ever be able to get back to their quiet life in her village?

CHAPTER 11
DECISIONS?

Yes, they did get back and at first Freya had seemed to be content, busy with her herb garden, and taking on again the care of the cow and goats and chickens. The winter months had passed quietly with spinning and weaving, keeping out the chill of the rainy season with the warm garments they had woven.

But now Maria was getting anxious. She stood at her cottage gate and called in vain for her Freya. 'She's off with the lads.' A neighbour wandered across to join her. 'She's like a pot of honey. All the boys are fighting over her, but she'll toss her curls and tease them. My grandson, Niko is moping around, all forlorn.'

Maria tried to change the subject, but as soon as she could she slipped back into her garden and taking a shovel she vented her frustration on her cabbage patch until at last, exhausted, she collapsed on the bench outside her door.

'My baby. How could this have happened? She is much too young to be setting up her own home and raising little ones.'

'Hey! Mama! Who is it that has upset you? I could see you arguing away.' One of her sons, now a father with his own farm, had called with a new born kid in his arms. 'A twin,' he explained later. 'We thought Freya might bottle feed it for us.'

But first he bent to embrace his mother then sat companionably beside her. 'Want to tell me about it?'

'No, not just now,' she whispered, for she had heard the sound of chatter as Freya was coming down from the hill, her escort of youths on her heels.

Freya gave her Nona a quick hug and a 'sorry,' then disappeared into the house. It wasn't long before food was on the table and they joined her inside, for a cool wind had sprung up.

It wasn't until Freya was out again on some mission Maria had given her that she was able to share her concern for her foster child with her now mature son.

'Yes, of course, she is much too young to think of marriage,' he agreed, 'but if she stays here, what else is there for her to do? I thought she was gifted in the spice trading?'

'Oh yes, she was, but Aba thought it best we come back to the village for a while. I wish I could talk to him, for our Freya is as much his responsibility as mine.'

It was a few weeks later that she heard her Freya shouting out, 'Nona, Nona! Aba, Aba is coming,' and she was running up the lane to meet him.

Greeting him joyfully, of course he had to be introduced to her kid, now thoroughly spoiled and getting under everyone's feet

After the excitement and catching up of family news, once again Freya was left to bring their ever- ready pot of stew to readiness while the adults sat out in the sunshine to talk.

CHAPTER 12
SPICE TRADERS IN EGYPT

The sea was calm, while a playful wind caught up the waves into tiny breakers skipping over the surface of the blue sea.

There had been long discussion all those months ago where they had been seated outside the cottage. First of all Maria had been able to explain to Antonio her concern for her foster child. Would it help to set out on another journey? And yet what of the fact that they had had to pack up in a hurry when it seemed that Freya's skills, as well as beauty, were causing too much attention?

Eventually they had called Freya in on the discussion. Yes, she felt it might be a good thing to distance herself from some of those moon struck youths, and even her pet kid must learn to go back to the herd. It seemed she was ready for more adventures.

Aba had sat there quietly, sucking on his beard. They heard the sound of voices wafting from the hills, and a shepherd piping to his flock. Freya had cleared away their bowls, poured Maria a glass of water and sat down, as much as to say, Come on Aba. We are ready to listen to you.

Now she and Maria were standing by the ship's rail. Her hair shimmered in the sunlight as the wind snatched it from her head covering.

'Aba had been afraid to suggest we make a sea crossing again,' Maria began, but when she saw the surprise on the girl's face, she changed the subject. Maybe her child had no memory of her tragic beginnings. After all, it was a long time ago.

'Egypt,' Freya murmured, after a while. 'I don't remember Aba even talking about Egypt before.'

Hearing mention of his name, the weather beaten old man came and joined them at the rail.

'Tell us about Egypt,' Freya asked. 'What made you think of going there?'

'Why, there have been new spices on the market, and they told me they were from Egypt. And there has been some wonderful new fabric too, Egyptian they say. I felt we were all ready for some new adventure…' he paused, and gave Maria's arm a friendly pat – 'and when I knew our Maria was willing, because I dare not take our Spice Maiden without her dragon to guard her, then I lifted up my eyes for new fields of treasure to explore.'

They had a calm crossing of the Great Sea, unloaded their mules and packs from the ship in the bustling port of Alexandria, then began a more gentle life as they travelled through some of the smaller towns that followed the life source of the Nile.

Maria was beginning to complain as their eyes searched yet another market. 'How can we do any trade?' she complained to Antonio. 'The further inland we go, the less we can make ourselves understood. And there are too many amorous eyes on our Freya…'

They had been plodding along a raised path, between some fields of flax and the River Nile, when suddenly, in the distance, Maria heard her Freya's voice.

'Freya!' she called. Where was she?

The girl ran up to them, obviously excited. 'Nona! Aba! It's there! The fragrance!'

They looked puzzled. They were not even approaching a market, but there was a cluster of white washed houses in the distance, and they had not long been passing a line of women waiting to draw water from a well.

'Frankincense?' Antonio asked her.

Freya looked puzzled. 'Frankincense?'

'Wasn't that what you smelled that led you to the Wise One?'

'I don't know. It was certainly part of his story.'

Their group was clustered around her now, excited, for they had all come to trust in Freya's sense of smell, but they were mystified too.

'Yes, there may have been a lingering perfume of frankincense, but I wouldn't have known about that if I had not become aware of this other fragrance which had seemed to be drawing me and leading me to this woman.

'Maybe it was something like the star that the Wise Ones had seen, leading them on until at last they saw the Holy Child?

'Oh, Nona, Aba,' and the sweep of her eyes included the rest of the Traders, for in a strange land it was important they all keep together. 'I must search for it.'

Antonio sighed, then pointed out a cluster of palm trees further along the embankment. 'We'll set up camp there for a few hours. Yes, time to prepare a meal,' he conceded to those who had become self- appointed cooks.

But Freya, dragging her poor Nona by the hand was returning to where she had seen the women, their water pots on their shoulders, or even upturned to make stools as they waited patiently for their turn to draw water.

Embarrassed, Maria gesticulated apologies with her hands as Freya, her senses quivering, walked quietly beside the women.

'Can we go now?' Maria had found a rock where she was waiting, watching and wondering where this would lead, when her Freya came and crouched down beside her.

'Well?' Maria queried.

Freya made a gesture with her nose towards a woman seated near the front of the queue, and who seemed to be helping to calm two restless children belonging to a younger woman.

'I'm sure she is the one,' she whispered. 'I'll wait until she has filled her jar and then we can offer to help her.'

'I don't know how you can make yourself understood,' Maria sniffed, but somehow this heavenly fragrance was filling her Freya with confidence. *Somehow,* she knew, they had been meant to come to Egypt.

The woman had handed over her responsibilities with the other children, and filled her pitcher. Freya had already run up and, her offer to carry it refused, had helped her to place her pad on the woman's head and then, lifting it between them it was settled for her to carry it to her house.

Once they were seated in the shade of a palm tree outside the little white washed dwelling and been refreshed with some slices of melon, Freya began to relate her story, of how she had been led to the home of the Wise One in Persia, and of his wonderful story of how he, with other Wise Ones had at last come to find the child, foretold by the stars and the ancient books and who had changed their lives.

She went on to tell her, 'When I passed you as you waited for water, I smelled a perfume, and I knew it was the very same perfume that had led me to meet with the Wise One and so to hear this story about the star that had led to them finding the Baby who was the King of the Jews.'

It was when Freya mentioned about the gift that he had brought of frankincense, the Egyptian woman became excited.

She sat quietly, then began to tell them her story. Once again there seemed to be a miracle in communication.

'A long time ago, a little family came to our village. They were refugees, from the land of Judea. Evidently there was a terrible king who would think nothing of slaughtering babies, and they thought their little boy was in danger. So they had left everything and eventually arrived here in our village. They had no money, but Joseph, the husband, had his bag of carpenters' tools, and yes, they did have some precious gifts that had been given them.'

She jumped up then and ran into the house. She returned with some cooling fruit juice for them to drink, but she had also brought out a jar with some granules of a certain fragrance inside. 'Frankincense,' she told them, and then went on to explain.

"We helped them when they first came, and let them sleep here. My old father, Achmed, was a carpenter, but he was struggling with his sight, - his eyes were growing milky with age, so he was glad to have Joseph, and was happy for them to move in with us.

"They gave us this little jar of frankincense to thank us for our kindness. I have kept this to remind me of this special family. But surely you did not smell this fragrance from my house?"

'"Tell me about the child," Freya asked her.

She was quiet for a while, then with tears in her eyes and awe in her voice, she began to speak.

'He was a wonderful child, just a sturdy little toddler, but always close to his Mother, not because she held him to her, but almost as if it was he who was caring for her. And in a way he seemed to be caring for us all. I remember one day I had anger in my heart towards my neighbour and I refused to respond to her greeting, turning away from her as we stood in the queue for water. Then I felt him as he slipped his little hand in mine, and then took the hand of my neighbour and gave us each such a sweet smile that we could not help but begin to laugh and of course I forgot all about the grudge I bore her.

'He seemed to be there for all of us. Oh, how we missed them, but the child especially, when they left us. I have so often thought of him, and longed that we might meet him again, although of course he will be grown by now; maybe working with his father as a carpenter, or even having taken over, for though his mother was young, about my age perhaps, his father was an older man."

That night as they set up camp, Maria was soon asleep, but Freya lay awake for a long time. Like her Egyptian friend she too longed to meet this wonderful Baby, Child, and by now surely young man – a carpenter maybe and yet – wonderful in every aspect of his life and undoubtedly King, as had been revealed by the stars and still being revealed by the fragrances of heaven.

And still they were continuing their search, for all these new spices they were discovering as well as the fine linens, were surely all meant for royalty. Where would they be led next?

CHAPTER 13
DETOUR TO DAMASCUS

Over the years Maria had come to take it for granted that with the coming of Spring there would be a message from Antonio, captain of the Spice Traders, and she knew it was time to arrange to have her little cottage boarded and to take leave of their neighbours, as well as handing over some responsibilities to her family. Not many of Freya's admirers remained to grieve over her departure, for several, realising they needed to lower their sights if they were to have a secure marriage, had already homes and farms of their own, while Maria, and Antonio too, were coming to understand that soon there would be no way they could continue to pass their beautiful Freya off as a boy. As it was, he tried to make sure that she was always securely guarded.

Year after year these intrepid spice traders set out with the arrival of Spring to travel to various lands. Maria might gladly have embraced a more settled life style, but she knew her beautiful Freya was always ready for more adventures, for there was a hunger in her heart, and it was not just for adventure or even riches; she had had a taste of a joy that was richer and deeper than any of the discoveries of new fragrances or spices.

'Where are we bound this time Aba?' But their Aba was not forthcoming. Perhaps he wasn't sure himself? Unless they were heading north, they would have to take ship to leave their homeland, Greece.

They had tramped their way through the small towns and ports on the coast until they reached a busy port where they marvelled at the array of smaller fishing vessels but also some larger ships that might even have sailed beyond the confines of their Great Sea. Yes, the captain would take their intrepid band aboard, claiming that they were set to reach the far Eastern lands.

Freya had long lost her fear of the sea, and even her Maria was enjoying the southern winds caressing her cheeks and filling the billowing sails so that the oarsmen had an easy time of it. The weather seemed set fair and the spice traders were planning to maybe leave the ship at Ephesus, but that was until the wind changed direction.

Antonio joined the captain at the helm. 'Are we going to make Ephesus?' he shouted, struggling to make himself heard.

'Ephesus?' Eventually he found breath between the sudden gusts. 'We've left it far behind. This wind has a mind of its own. Maybe the island of Crete?

You could do some trading there, for it is said to be the source of many treasures.'

Maria had gone below decks and was lying on a pile of empty sacking, while her Freya was busy caring for her. By the time her Nona was well enough to come back on deck, Freya was able to go to enquire where they were bound.

'Crete? We've been blown well south of the island.' Antonio passed on the Captain's news to the rest of his party. 'It looks as if we are likely to reach to the port of Sidon, in Lebanon.'

'Sidon, Sidon?' The questions were banded to and fro.

Antonio waited until he had his own little band gathered around him. 'It looks as if the gods are prospering us,' he whispered, 'for it seems Sidon, and Tyre too is a port of great wealth and wonderful treasures.'

'And fragrance?' asked Freya.

'Who knows?' But another traveller had heard her question, and finding himself standing next to the 'youth' as he thought, as they stood viewing the port in the distance, he spoke to her quietly.

'If you are searching for fragrance, you should make for the city of Jerusalem. They say that the Jews, as they call them, use the most wonderful fragrances in all the world in connection with their Temple worship.'

'Oh, thank you, thank you.' Freya was excited as she shared the information with Antonio. But he sucked on his beard a little before answering.

'We'll see. We'll see.'

But once they had landed and begun exploring the markets with so many wonders on display and many others hidden away until they found out if they were prepared to negotiate with high prices or not, no one seemed to have any interest in going any further, and when they were at last ready to move on, it was Damascus they were heading for. Even Freya seemed to have no more thought of Jerusalem.

'Oh, such fragrance! Maria! Maria! Oh, is it the air? Where does it come from?'

Even her Maria was alert to it, while others, aware of Freya's interest, gathered around her, so many wanting to tell her more.

It was an older man who demanded the right to inform her, and chased away all lesser mortals.

'Come,' he commanded. 'It is jasmine. I will show you. You have done well to come to Damascus, for this is known as the city of jasmine.'

Freya's guards had quickly called Antonio, so that he was one of the party as they were led through the cobbled streets to where there was an ancient wall covered in a blanket of this wonderful aromatic shrub, with the delicately petalled flower.

Their guide was busy arguing with the old man, for he could see that the lad, as he thought, was the one aware of the value of the fragrance, but was in no position to negotiate any business.

'Come!' Maria took her firmly by the hand. 'Aba says we must come. We don't want to draw attention to ourselves. He'll make sure we have a cutting to pack away carefully.'

Freya followed unwillingly, but the fragrance had permeated their garments and, obliterating any unpleasant smells that usually accompany crowded places, seemed to be in the air around them.

Maria meanwhile was enchanted by some of the costly garments that were on display, but one of their party whispered to her, 'Make the most of all the sights, for Aba is anxious to make tracks for Jerusalem.'

They had found a quiet place to set up their camp, - quiet, yet safe, for it was within the shadow of the walls of the ancient city, and Freya slept peacefully with the fragrance of the jasmine still in her nostrils.

Maria had already fetched water from the well so that Freya could get washed and dressed. She was afraid she might be unwilling for them to move on, enchanted as she had been by the fragrance of the jasmine, and she seemed to be in some sort of trance.

'Freya, what is it?'

'I, I think it might have been a dream.'

'Well?' Maria waited, trying to be patient. 'Aba will be angry if we keep him waiting.'

'No, it is alright Maria. I will get ready quickly, but I thought there was someone speaking to me – it must have been through the tent wall.'

'Yes?' Maria was handing her a towel, and then her garments even as they talked. 'What did he say?'

'He said, what someone else had said when we first landed, about that the most precious fragrance was to be found in Jerusalem.'

CHAPTER 14
JERUSALEM

Freya, as usual, a spring in her step, was drinking in all the sights and sounds as, having made a reluctant farewell from Damascus, once more they were journeying on. She was learning to trust in her dreams and impulses. Through the voice in her sleep her hunger for the heavenly fragrance had been reawakened and she felt sure now that Jerusalem would bring some rich reward.

But her dear Maria was struggling. While each year that passed since her Freya had been committed to her care had brought new strength, and joy too, each day bringing new adventures for her adopted, year by year, and journey by journey, yet now poor Maria was feeling her strength waning, her bones creaking a little more and her poor feet complaining.

As Antonio checked up on each one in his little band he too was becoming aware that this was not the sprightly Maria who had been so happy to give a home and her heart to their little orphan. He waited for a quiet moment to draw her apart.

'This may be the last journey we make together,' he assured her, 'I can see you are ready for a quieter life back in your village.'

Maria snorted. 'I may be, yes, but you'll not pen up our lassie, and who would guard her as I do?'

Antonio drew nearer, and looked around to make sure they were not being over-heard. Another party of traders were gathering around the well where they were resting but they had no interest in their conversation.

Reassured, he continued.

'It's time she had a husband to care for her, Maria: time for us to pass on our responsibilities.'

Shocked, Maria began to splutter out objections. But Aba continued.

'Of course we must make sure she has a good marriage, Maria. I've been on the look- out for a while now, but there is only one who I felt might have been good enough. Remember the young prince we met when we were in Persia? Of course she was much too young then ...'

'And much too useful to you,' Maria interjected.

'Don't interrupt, Woman,' Antonio snapped. He was feeling the nagging of old age himself, which made him cross. 'It has been obvious that we would have to make a good match for her, even from the beginning.'

He fingered the pouch he always carried around his neck, and Maria realised he had never parted with the precious jewelled locket he had taken from the neck of the dead woman – presumably Freya's mother. 'Yes,' he assured her. 'I'm sure this would make a more than adequate bride price, should it be demanded, but we want someone who would see the great value she is of herself.'

The others were loading up their mules, and Antonio checked to make sure there was a beast, well padded, to carry Maria, and give her feet a rest. But Freya seemed to have a fresh spring in her step the nearer they were to Jerusalem. It wasn't just her search for this fragrance, but now and again, as they mingled with the crowds, she heard the whisper of a certain name, a name she had heard from the lips of the Wise One in Persia, and again in the village by the Nile, in the land of Egypt. Yes, 'Jesus'. That was it, the name of Jesus. But how was it people seemed to be talking about him now? Could it be the same Jesus?

And what was the matter with her dear Maria? She seemed so cross and fretful, angry if a lock of her golden hair should slip from beneath her head covering, or if she strayed far from her side.

But oh, Freya's heart was stirred as at last they were within sight of this city they were seeking, Jerusalem.

CHAPTER 15
CITY OF GOD?

Somehow Freya was not aware of the beauty of the City of God, as many seemed to call the ancient citadel of Jerusalem, as they climbed ever upward to reach it. Sometimes she felt as if she could not breathe for the pressure of the throng that was swelling around them, though Antonio had made sure that their own Spice Traders kept close together so that it was those of her own party who were always hemming them in.

How was it that so many had decided to make this journey at the same time? It was Antonio again who, keeping his ear to the ground, explained to them that Easter time, as they had heard it called, was a special festival for the Jews, and though, since the Romans had made the possibility of travel so much more feasible, many had scattered to make their homes in other lands, their religion still demanded their attendance in their Mother city and especially to come to their Temple for this yearly feast of Passover.

'When, and how do we get to the Temple?' Freya asked, as the old Spice Trader tried to gather his company around him. She was aware only of the odours accompanying poverty and pollution. Where were these spices and perfumes they had been promised?'

'They do say these Jews keep this as a closely guarded secret,' one of the older traders spoke up.

'And they don't exactly welcome 'Gentiles' as they call us.'

'And women certainly are not allowed in,' volunteered another.

'Let's leave that until tomorrow.' Their Aba spoke with authority. 'We need to find somewhere to set up our tents.' Taking Maria aside, he suggested that she take Freya and see if she could find a welcome in one of the nearby villages.

The sun was setting when the little band reached a cluster of houses. The youths, who always were more than willing to act as guard to Freya, had walked a few miles with them until they had come to a quiet little town. They had wanted to stay with them, but the ubiquitous Maria assured them that they were no longer necessary and that they should return to join the others.

'We will wait to see you are welcomed and then will join the others and come again to find you in the morning.'

Freya could feel Maria shaking as she took firm hold of her arm.

'The Jews pray to their God,' Freya whispered. 'Do you think he would hear us if we asked him to guide us to a friendly home?'

'Goodness me, how should I know? You do it if you think he would listen to us.'

But before she had pondered how to do this, Freya began to take determined footsteps between some huddled houses, passing the fig tree that seemed a place of welcome for travellers in the heat of the day but of no comfort now, but then to another cluster of houses. All the time poor Maria was clinging, mystified, to her arm.

'What….?' She tried to ask, but Freya was explaining.

'The fragrance, Maria. Don't you smell it? I think it is here, in this dwelling. Come, let us knock. Don't be afraid.' Firmly she knocked upon the gate.

'I might have known,' grumbled Maria. 'You were like a hound on the hunt. Dragging me along with my poor weary feet, and now all I can smell is the aroma of the vegetable stew they are cooking.'

'Yes, I'm sure it is a delicious stew, but it was not this that had attracted me. Shh. They are coming.'

It was a child who had been sent to open the gate. Seeing them she called to her mother and it wasn't long before they were invited in, seated around their table and sharing their supper. The mother of the family explained to them about the feast and that tomorrow they intended to go into the city, but all the time Freya was aware of the fragrance. Somehow she was beginning to understand that it was for this that she had been spared and rescued after the terrible storm and shipwreck; for this she had been forced, as it were, to turn aside to meet with the Wise One, in the land of Persia; and then again in that village by the Nile, in the land of Egypt. And now, here they were in the land of Judah, and surely they had been led to share a meal with this family, but how, how could she find the answer to the searching of her heart?

After the meal the matron of the family directed their visitors to the shade of the fig tree. 'You go and sit there and talk to my mother while we prepare you sleeping accommodation. She has a story she would love to share with you.'

Freya, Maria too, sat beside the woman. Her face was wrinkled, as if she were very old, though they sensed that maybe she was not, but her face lit up now with a smile that was like a lamp lighting up a dark house.

They waited awhile for her to speak, but she just sat there as if enjoying her memories. 'Tell me,' Freya asked at last, 'Have you met him, this wonderful person?' 'Yes, oh yes,' she nodded, but then seemed to lean again into her memories.

Eventually her daughter, having finished her chores, came and joined them.

'Shall I tell them your story, Mother?' she asked. Her mother nodded happily. She radiated peace.

'When I was a little girl we lived in Bethlehem,' her daughter began, 'It was at the time when the Romans decreed that everyone had to come to their own city to pay their taxes. It was chaos at the time, but then many who had travelled had returned to their homes, but there was one very special family who had come to pay their taxes. Their child was born while they were there and so they stayed on for a while. It was we children who were the first to realise that somehow they were a very special family. We heard stories from the shepherds of angels singing, but it was when these strange wise men came from far away lands in the East that somehow we sensed amazement, but also - that trouble was brewing.

'We wanted to go and ask them more about the baby, and why these important people had come, but when we went to the house, they were gone. Nobody knew where.'

'Egypt, maybe?' Maria whispered. Freya nodded, but the mother was wiping a tear from her eye before she continued.

'It wasn't many days after that King Herod's soldiers came to our quiet little town. 'The King demands the boy child recently born here.'

She, and her mother too, was weeping as she continued.

'Of course, we did not know where this special one was, and if we had known we would not have told, but oh. Those soldiers went mad, raging like lions through the town, searching for all the boy babies, even up to two years old. I, and the older children, had run to hide in the corn, but when eventually we crept out and I came home, I found Mother holding the body of my little brother in her arms. Yes, they had slashed his little throat. I was screaming and clinging to him too.

'Eventually neighbours came and forced my mother to let them take his body and bury him.'

They were all weeping now –family and visitors alike, and Miriam, the daughter telling them the story, held her mother close and assured her, 'This isn't the end of the story, is it Mother?'

''You see little Anna over there?' Miriam pointed out a little child, seeking to help to wash the dishes. 'I was about her age when this happened, but I now had to become carer for my mother, and of course, all too soon I had grown and had my own family, but with an extra child to care for, for the tragedy had stolen my mother's mind.'

'But now?' Freya asked. It was the grandmother herself who eventually took up the tale.

'I was sitting with the children. –I used to spend most of the day sitting with the children. Miriam would tell me I was helping her, but I know now that I was just an extra burden. This day I had the baby on my knee when the Teacher came and gently held out his arms for me to place the baby in them. Then, holding the child he looked into my eyes.

''They stole your baby, didn't they?' he asked. A terrible memory, a memory I had buried deep into my subconscious, began to stir and large tears were pouring down my face.

'"Do you know your baby died so that I could be saved?" he told me. "Thank you, thank you, my daughter." Gently he placed the little one again in my arms and went on to speak, not so much to me, but to those who always seemed to gather around him. 'But I am yet to die, that your little ones may yet be restored to you.'

'"Now dry your eyes, dear Daughter."

'You did, didn't you, Mother?' Miriam asked.

'I did, I did.' There was such joy in her affirmation. 'Do you remember how he called you and all the little ones around us and the Teacher lifted up his arms and it was as if the sky had opened up and he was calling down blessings from heaven on us all.'

'Of course I remember, Mother, - we all do, don't we children?' and the children gathered joyfully around to confirm the story.

Freya lay awake for a long time that night. It seemed as if the fragrance was permeating even the blankets in which they were wrapped. How surely they had been led. Little by little she was becoming able to piece together the story of this Wonderful One who had come from heaven. And now, was it possible that they might even meet him? Now that he was a man, might it be possible that she herself could ever be in possession of this wonderful fragrance which could only have come from heaven?

CHAPTER 16
TO SEE JESUS?

After a breakfast of bread and figs, their hosts arranged for a neighbour's son to accompany their visitors into the city and hopefully help them to locate the rest of their company, for there was no sign of their promised escort.

It was a beautiful fresh Spring morning. Trees were in blossom along the road side and crocuses lined the banks. Freya had a song of joy in her heart for she knew that now, at last there was the possibility of meeting this Jesus, who must surely be the one sent from heaven. But as they entered within the precincts of the city of Jerusalem the fragrance seemed to be fading from her memory and other odours began to press around her.

There were the piping voices of little children with cages of sparrows to sell. It took older boys to carry large jars of water, offering a drink to those who were thirsty. As the sun rose higher they would soon make good sales.

Cattle were being driven past them, leaving muck in their paths, and later they found themselves surrounded by a flock of sheep.

'They are taking them to the temple for the people to buy for their sacrifice,' their guide volunteered, and just then he was able to point out to them a glimpse of this magnificent building that seemed to be glinting gold in the morning sun. Freya wanted to make her way there, - was it not there that the wonderful perfumes were offered to their God?

'Best find Aba first,' Maria warned to Freya, and gave the youth what directions she could remember, and it wasn't long before they were found by one of their own band.

Freya was wanting to share her excitement, for her hosts had assured her that the same Jesus who had healed the grandmother was likely to be coming up to Jerusalem for the feast, but Maria cautioned her to save her breath, for the narrow streets seemed to be growing ever more crowded and they needed to keep a close hold on each other.

At last they clambered through part of an olive grove into an open hillside where groups had set up their tents and had some measure of privacy.

Antonio seemed so thankful to see Maria with their precious Freya brought back to them, but strangely he did not appear very concerned to listen to the story Freya wanted to share with him. It seemed he too had a story. At last he had all of his little band fed and watered and settled around him and he began his tale.

'You remember, as we journeyed toward Jerusalem from Damascus, we realised that we were among many who were Jews returning to their own land for the special Springtime feast, Passover they call it?'

Freya turned to Maria, wanting to share her excitement in realising that it was because it was this special time of festivity that there had been the expectation of this one, Jesus, and that his name was on so many lips, but Aba's stern eyes silenced her, and she soon became aware that he too had a contribution to this wonderful story. Of how great importance she was soon to realise.

'I had been conversing with one of these travellers who had heard so much about this Jesus that our Freya has already heard about.' He turned, nodding approvingly to their Spice Maiden before he continued.

'He told me that a cousin of his had become a follower of this Jesus; the Master as they call him. He's been travelling around the country with him and has come home with wonderful stories to tell.'

'Yes?' Maria interrupted. How could this story be more important than the one their Freya had to share? But Aba's glare silenced her.

'Oh, why are women so impatient?' he complained. 'Listen to this, our Freya, and see if you do not think this of more importance than any of your stories that you have gathered over the years.'

Freya was kneeling beside their Aba now, as if she would take the words out of his mouth, while Maria hushed a lad whose attention had been diverted by some passing trader.

'I met this man this morning. His name is Simeon. He told me that he had heard that they did not think his cousin would be coming to the feast, which is this coming weekend, because the authorities are so angry because all the common people think so much of his Master, Jesus, that they have been warned to lie low for a bit.'

Freya looked at Maria in dismay. Somehow she had thought that the longings of her heart were to be fulfilled. Were they to be dashed again?

'Oh women! Women!' Antonio muttered, 'Will you not trust that I have something worth telling?'

Again they waited upon him in expectation.

'Simeon came back to find me and he whispered to me that yes, his cousin, Philip is his name, has indeed come. He told me a long story too of how the

44

people gave him a wonderful welcome and his Master is certainly not in hiding, but yes – I'm coming to the good news for us. Simeon had told his cousin of how we so desired to see this Jesus, and he is going to ask him if he will agree to meet with us.'

'Oh Aba! Aba! When? Did he agree? When? Where?'

'Simeon showed me the place where Andrew had suggested that we wait, soon after sunrise tomorrow, so ….. you have a day to do any trading, or whatever. We will camp here again tonight.'

'Yes, yes, our friends are happy for us to return to them for as long as we are in the city,' Maria assured him, when he enquired about their accommodation.

Meanwhile Freya was overwhelmed with a sense of joy and hope. It was as if she was reaching a peak in her life and that tomorrow she would find that all the adventures this far had been for this one purpose. Oh, how blessed we are that the future is not as yet an open book.

CHAPTER 17

A GREAT HOPE

Freya had thought that she would not be able to sleep for excitement, for was she not about to meet with this One who had previously made himself known to her through this most exquisite of all fragrances?

Washed and dressed, she slipped out into the courtyard.

She would have set out with the awakening of the birds, but she knew of course that she must not go without her Maria, and also the guides who had been promised them. Suppose they set out to see Jesus, but were left wandering about unable to find him?

It was the grandmother who brought out a dish of grapes and sat quietly beside her as they shared them.

'You are going to meet with the Master?' she asked at last.

'Oh, yes, yes. Philip said he would ask him. Surely he won't say no?'

'What about you? If he asks you to follow him, will you say no?'

Freya paused, wondering. 'But I am a girl. Would he want a girl to follow him?'

'Why not? I know a woman who follows him wherever he goes. I understand why this woman, Mary, won't leave him, for she was an outcast. Everyone shunned her, except those vile fellows who abused her, but there are also other respectable women, some of them rich, who follow him and help to look after him. The men who follow him, his disciples, don't mind, for they provide food and other needs and comforts for them all.'

Maria was ready now and a couple of their young men had come to lead them safely into the city, and to the tree just near the olive grove where they had agreed to meet up.

Oh, what a jostle and a hustle there was, once they were within the boundaries of the city. The young men had taken Freya and Maria by their arms for fear they might become separated. 'Look!' one exclaimed. 'The Temple!' But they only had a flash of gold as the sun caught its pinnacle and it was hidden again by the crowds.

'Look! There is Aba!' Maria exclaimed. They continued their struggle through the surging crowds. Once or twice they caught a glimpse of Aba and some of his party and then, at last, they felt themselves, pulled like a storm tossed boat into a haven, and there were Niko, Petros and others of their little band of traders drawing them into their group as they clustered around Antonio.

Having rewarded their guides, Aba put two of his men to look out for Philip, while the rest of them retired into a quieter spot nearer to the gardens. But all of them were on the alert, for by now each one had a great expectation of seeing this wonderful one they called Jesus.

'Is he really in Jerusalem?' one of them asked. 'Didn't someone on the road say that he would not dare to come because of his enemies?'

'No, no. He is definitely here,' affirmed another. 'Did you not notice all those branches torn from the palm trees and still lying on the side of the road leading up to the temple? They told me that the people were so excited when they saw that Jesus was indeed coming that they put him on a donkey – the men threw their coats to make a carpet for him and they were waving the palm branches as they would welcome a mighty conqueror.'

'But I thought someone said he had enemies? They wouldn't have been too happy at that?'

At the first mention of enemies Freya had felt a terrible heaviness grip her stomach, and when she saw Simeon with Philip slip through their group to speak with Antonio, she began to tremble with fear.

What darkness was this that was descending on her?

CHAPTER 18
A GREAT FEAR

Philip tried to reassure them that it was not an out and out rejection that his Master had given to their request. He had told Jesus that they were a respectable band of merchants, yes, from Greece.

'Jesus said something about a grain of corn being useless unless it is buried in the earth to die, and that only if it dies can it bring forth, perhaps a hundred more grains, or even more. But it was as if he had more important things to do.'

'What was he saying? We don't understand.' They sat around, puzzling over those strange words, like dogs might worry over a bone, until at last Freya spoke out. She was talking quietly to Maria, close beside her, but her voice carried and she found they were all listening

'A grain of corn has to be buried in the earth, but we just have to wait then until it starts to send up a green shoot, and then more waiting for it to fill out and ripen. What can that have to do with him not agreeing to see us? I feel as if I have been waiting all my life to see this Jesus.

'And why is he talking about dying? It cannot be. Why, the Wise Ones saw his star in the heavens, and it led them to find him as a baby, and now the people have welcomed him in triumph, and there are so many people he has healed.'

Others butted in now with stories they had heard of his miracles and healings.

'He may have enemies, but he surely has hundreds, if not thousands more of his friends who would rise up to protect him.'

The talk swirled to and fro, but Maria cried out in fear, for Freya had curled herself up into a ball, her cloth wrapped around her head.

'I can't bear it, I can't bear it,' she moaned. 'I've been following, no not a star, but somehow the trail of his fragrance all my life. I can't bear to wait any more.'

Poor Maria sat, helpless, beside this one who had become almost more than a daughter to her. Freya seemed to be out of her mind, flinging her limbs about and even her Maria could not get near to comfort or help.

'Oh, if only this Jesus had come, this would not have happened,' one of the men grumbled, while one of the younger lads offered to go and seek this Teacher, for was he not a healer?

'And where would you go to find him? Do you know where he is? And if he would not come when Philip, his friend, asked him, is he likely to come now?'

Just then Maria came up with an idea. She pulled Aba aside. They talked in low voices until at last Aba called for attention.

'Maria is willing to return to the village where they have found a safe place to stay. She wants to go to seek the woman who has been so wonderfully healed by this Jesus to ask her to come and pray with our Freya, or even maybe she could go and beg the Master to come to her.'

Rather than sit helplessly, not knowing what to do, and with the two willing lads to accompany her she set out again on that long walk back to the village. Poor dear Maria! Nothing was too much trouble for the sake of her Freya, but if she had known what would happen before she would return, would she have ever left her?

CHAPTER 19
A GREAT DARKNESS

It was a day or two later, and getting towards evening when a troubled Maria eventually returned to where she had left the little band of Spice Traders, but not surprisingly there seemed to be no sign of them. The elderly woman felt like withdrawing from life as her adopted child had done, but if she were to wrap herself up like a cocoon, or even fling herself to the ground in despair, then who would care for her Freya?

And where was her Freya? She sat down on a rock, for she did not know where to begin to search. Surely someone from their party would take pity on her and bring her some news.

It was Antonio who eventually came, a basket with some bread and fish in his hand which he offered poor, weary, yes, and frightened Maria. Her fear was expressed in anger. She pushed away his peace offering.

'If you want me to take you to her,' he coaxed, 'you'd best eat or I'll have you ill as well as our maiden, and I'll have to hire a bier to carry you too.

'There is nothing the matter with my legs,' she snapped at him, as she handed him back a now empty basket.

'Nor your tongue either,' he teased, yet giving her an arm to steady her over some rough stones. 'Now, promise not to interrupt and I'll tell you where we are going.'

She nodded her assent, but even so they had walked a way, up through the olive groves to the less crowded ground where a large encampment had been set up, before he found his courage to speak.

'After you had set out, and not long gone, people were beginning to gather around to see what was going on, and of course, that was the last thing we needed. But then a man of some importance approached me.

''Excuse me, but my master has his encampment further up the hillside. He heard of your distress and he offers his hospitality. We have place where the young woman could rest in quietness and have the care she needs until she is recovered.'

'So is she there?'

'Yes, I am taking you there. But what about your friend in the village? Was she willing to come with you?'

Maria shook her head. 'I was delayed on the way. There was a young woman in labour and her mother in great distress. I could not leave them without staying to help until her child was safely born. And when at last we did get to their village they were not there. The house was shut up. It seems they too have come to the City for the Feast, and in hope of seeing the Master again. Have you sent our men to seek for him? But even if they found him, we don't know if he would be willing to come. Perhaps he would tell them again about the corn of wheat having to die? Oh dear, we don't want any more talk about dying.'

Antonio made no effort to answer her many questions but left Maria to do all the talking as they walked quietly up to the encampment. Before they should call out, the same messenger who had first been sent to Antonio came out, his finger to his lips and beckoned them inside.

Freya lay on a divan, covered only with a light linen cloth, while a servant knelt near her head, fanning her, and another was dabbing cold water on her brow.

'Freya, oh my Freya!' Maria ran to embrace her, but there was no response or sign of recognition from their Spice Maiden, only troubled muttering and gesticulations. Another woman, of about Maria's age, held her back and gently led her to sit on a bench nearby.

'Are you her mother?' she asked.

Maria could only shake her head, for she was overcome by tears. Eventually the other woman gently took Maria by the arm and led her out of the tent to walk in the shade of the olive trees. It was not until many months later and in what seemed to be another life that Maria learned that her name was Prisca.

'My Master is the Prince Hermas. He too has followed the trail of the Spice Traders, though this time he is seeking a greater treasure. But what strange fate has brought us together here on this Holy Mount?

'But be assured that if anyone is able to help your child, he is. He wills only good for her.'

Maria felt confused and ill at ease. There were many things she could not understand and wanted to ask this gentle lady, but her heart was with her Freya, and somehow, for some strange reason, she had an uneasiness with regard to Antonio. Through the long years since he brought the little toddler to her care she had always had a nagging doubt that all his care for her would turn out to be to his benefit.

Prisca was suggesting that they sit awhile, but Maria insisted that they return again to where her Freya lay, troubled and struggling. She was in foetal position now, the sheet pulled over her head, sometimes mumbling but occasionally shouting out as if in great pain.

She had noted Antonio deep in conversation with the one Maria was to eventually learn was the Prince. It was his voice that carried now to the anxious Maria.

'I have my servants with their ears to the ground to find out what is going on in the city. If only we could assure the maiden that the Master, Jesus, is not in danger, and that there is still hope of her meeting him, that this would effect her cure, but I'm afraid the news is not good. It seems the religious leaders are determined to get him. He is still preaching in the temple, but no one seems to know where he is staying.'

Maria noted then how Antonio seemed to seek to turn the Prince so that they could not be overheard before he spoke with him at some length. It looked like a nod of affirmation from the Prince before he turned away and called another of his servants.

She returned now to this one who was perhaps more than a daughter to her. Her carers made room so that she could sit beside her, but Freya seemed entirely unaware of her presence and continued to moan and thrash around, as if in great pain.

Antonio had followed her in and came near as if to offer comfort, but Maria had been aware of his glance in her direction, almost of triumph, and she would not allow herself to trust him. But who could she trust? And where could they go for any help? Oh, if only there were better news of this one whom many said was the Jew's Messiah, and surely not just of the Jews, for it seemed her Freya had set all her hope in him.

It was strange how they had seemed, as a group, to have been so drawn to this city, but oh, now Jerusalem appeared to be such a dark place, a darkness that was closing in on them.

CHAPTER 20
HOPE OF HEALING?

Maria felt a cooling breeze as she walked alone through the olive trees. Oh, where could she turn for any comfort? She felt so very alone.

But soon she realised she was not alone. Dear Prisca, this loving, motherly servant of the Prince, had come to walk beside her. Maria turned to acknowledge her and, noting the tears ready to brim over, slipped her arm around her waist.

They walked in companionable silence, Prisca wisely waiting for this heart-broken woman to speak first.

'We were so excited to come here to Jerusalem. We were told that this was the place where the most fragrant spices and perfumes were offered to their God. But all we found was great walls that excluded women and foreigners and all we could hear was the cry of helpless sheep being driven to the slaughter and the only smells the ugly stench of blood.'

Prisca let Maria talk, then gently asked, 'Was it this which has caused such heart breaking disappointment for your Freya?'

Maria was quiet for a while before she spoke.

'No, it was more than that.' They had found the stump of an ancient olive tree that had been left as a resting place for the weary. Maria began to recount how this beautiful little child put in her care had always had an awareness of fragrance and perfume, and how it had seemed to lead her on to hear stories of this one, Jesus until now she had thought that she was actually to meet with him.

'And did you not go to see him? From what I have heard of him he does not turn people away.'

The tears were now flowing from Maria's eyes and she told of the strange message Philip had brought them.

'And since then the world seems to be getting darker and darker, and I really fear that some terrible tragedy is about to come on this city, and that our Freya may die of a broken heart.'

They wept together for a while, and then Prisca spoke.

'Did you remember ever seeing the Prince Hermas before?' Bewildered, Maria shook her head.

'It was in Persia I believe. He had seen your Freya yet, though she was not then fully grown his heart went out to her and he approached your Antonio concerning marriage, but he insisted she was far too young and maybe when she was older.'

'Oh!' Maria was pondering, recalling the time he had said they should try to disguise her as a lad.

'The Prince was not convinced that it was only for the good of Freya, but maybe it was for his own advantage that he had refused.' Maria nodded her agreement. She had never felt she could completely trust the old trader.

'So?' she questioned.

'Your leader had made sure our Prince could not follow your party, but now it seems, by some strange fate, your paths have crossed again, and he was here at the time of your Freya's great need.'

'Oh yes indeed,' Maria agreed. 'Your care of us all has been wonderful, but surely he would not want her as a wife, now in this condition. Antonio could not expect a bride price from him now?'

'Oh certainly, yes. It is his desire to take her as his wife, if only she will regain enough consciousness to give her consent. And he is more than willing to pay a high bride price. But it seems that now your Antonio is willing to give him a gift of great value if only we would take her off his hands.'

Maria jumped up. Her eyes were blazing now.

'Oh that rogue! That rogue! I see it now. He was willing to let her go, without even telling me, because he knew I would not be willing.'

Prisca was standing too, her arms around her friend, pleading, coaxing. 'Come, come, Maria, your love for your child is great enough for this. For all of us there comes a time when we must be willing to let our children go. And she will have a husband who is not only rich but good and who loves her deeply and truly.'

Another servant came, maybe Prisca's husband from the confident way he placed his arm around her before joining the conversation.

'And you should see the beauty of the island kingdom that our Prince will inherit, now that his father is satisfied that he has at last found a bride after his own heart. No place for darkness there. Your Freya will surely find healing for herself, and for many others too.'

Could this be true? Was there indeed to be a happy ending for her Spice maiden? But what of her dear Maria?

PART 2 – FREYA'S FRAGRANCE
CHAPTER 1
IN SEARCH OF HER SPICE MAIDEN

As Maria put down her bundle and paused to wipe her face, she heard a gentle piping. The melody was sweet, haunting. At first she thought it must have come from the heavens, but as she looked upwards she espied a goat herd up in the hills and realised it was he who was making music with his little pipe while his flock were grazing around him. The woman laughed gently to herself. 'You are getting like your little Spice Maiden,' she chided herself, 'thinking everything comes to you especially from heaven.'

The melody continued to flow down the hillside as a refreshing stream, while a gentle breeze wafted a fragrance from the vineyard she was passing. Weary from the steep climb up from the coast, Maria sank down onto a grassy bank.

Was she foolish to have made this long journey? Maybe Freya, her little Spice Maiden, as they had all affectionately come to call her, would have forgotten about her Nona. Or maybe with this great change in her circumstances, no longer travelling as part of the entourage of Old Antonio and his spice merchants but now married to a rich landowner, she would not want to recognise her? And yet she had had this persistent nagging that this child who, for so long, she had taken to her bosom as her own, was in need of her.

They had parted in such terrible circumstances: her Freya so overwrought with all the darkness around her that she seemed to be in some sort of coma, while with terrible predictions of tragedy all around her, it seemed this offer from the Prince of swift transport out of Jerusalem was the only possibility.

Indeed, the gloom and forebodings in Jerusalem, and the rumour that this Jesus had been arrested was enough to have caused her too, yes, Freya's strong village nona from Greece to be near to losing her senses too when Antonio had called them all to pack up and take flight, making for the coast as swiftly as possible; not that any travel in those days could be thought of as swift.

Maria must have fallen asleep, she had no idea for how long, but she was awakened by the sound of the flap of sandals on the stony path, and the next moment she was struggling to get to her feet while she was being smothered in a strong embrace.

'Oh Nona, my own Nona!' and they were there, together again. She, the adopted grandmother and this precious child who had been thrust upon her when she had thought her time for child rearing was long past.

'Mercy, mercy,' she cried, at last able to stand. 'Now then, let me look at you.' Her mother heart took in at once that all was not well with this beautiful woman who stood before her, for it was not just tears of joy that she was shedding.

'But… how did you know I was on my way?'

'Oh, it was Justus, the goat herd. I was tending my herb garden and he ran to tell me a stranger was approaching. We don't often get strangers on this part of the island, and when he said it was a woman, I wondered if somehow you had felt the great longing that was in my heart for you…. and – here you are.' Her tears were welling up again, but they walked on until they had reached the shade of a grove. Soft turf was beneath their feet now as she led her friend to a sheltered bower where Maria could sit and rest while Freya went to the house, calling for one of the servants to bring refreshment.

They sat in silence for a while, drinking the goat's milk and feasting on the luscious peaches which had been freshly plucked. Maria sat quietly, wise enough to know she must wait until her Freya wanted to talk.

'How is old Antonio? Is he off on another of his expeditions? Is he still determined to go East? But how is it you are not with them?' At last Freya's questions began to tumble out.

'Why, I am of no use to them without our Spice Maiden. I was only dragged along to take care of you. It is you they wanted, for you always seemed to be aware of some new fragrance, or a different spice or seasoning.'

'And yet he gave me away?' Maria sensed the hint of bitterness in the girl's tone.

'Well, hardly gave you away. The young prince, your husband, had to pay him a great bride price, in order to have you. And Aba knew it was time for you to be married. We had dressed you as a lad when you were younger, feeling this would keep you safe, but now your beauty could no longer be hid. It was time for you to marry, and he must have felt sure the prince would love and cherish you.'

'Oh yes, he loves and cherished me.' Maria, again noting the bitterness in her voice, was determined to know more, but waited for Freya to continue. 'I guess Aba bragged my gift at recognising fragrances, and so he married me thinking I was going to make him rich. As if he isn't rich enough already.' she added, as if to herself.

'See these gardens, planted out with every known herb and flower? I will show you the sheds where we distil the oils – but…' Maria stretched out her arms to the girl but she ignored her offer of comfort, even though she was struggling with her emotions. After a while she raised her head.

'Oh Maria, - I am so afraid. I think I have lost my skill and he won't want me anymore.'

'Of course he will want you. How could any man not love you? But tell me, what makes you think you have lost your skill, for it is surely a gift from the gods. Why, as a tiny tot you ran after anyone with the scent of myrrh, thinking it might be your mother.

'Old Aba had this locket of myrrh. As soon as you smelled it, you reacted, calling for your mother, but he didn't give it to you.' Maria was reverting to the familiar name she had known him by before he had taken on this roman sounding name which he hoped sounded more impressive. Antonio, or Aba, which seemed much more familiar, and indeed, as Maria had taken the identity of mother, so Antonio, as Aba, took the role of father.

'No. He told me, he was afraid someone might snatch it from you, or even take you with it, thinking someone might come to search for you and demand a ransom. 'I'll keep it safe, I promise,' he told me.

'Yes, he says he gave it to my husband,' Freya confirmed, 'and had told him to guard it for me, so it seems I am never to be trusted with it. Or,' and here Freya paused and then, as if this was a fresh idea, 'Is it that they don't want me to know anything about my mother?'

Still weary from her journey, Maria closed her eyes. She felt, as she had so often felt it before in her imaginings. She could hear the roar of the breakers, the screaming of the wind in the rigging and a great sense of fear as the timbers of the vessel trembled in the terrible storm.

As Freya rose to slip quietly away, realising her friend's need to sleep, Maria stirred. No, they had not had a rough passage as the boat had brought her on this visit. So why did she have this persistent dream? Watching the girl making her way to the veranda of the fine mansion of which she was now mistress, Maria's sense of unease would not leave her. All was not well with the young woman. Where was the feisty young girl she had reared, grown from the fretful child that had been thrust into her arms? This was the one they had eventually decided to dress as a boy, feeling she was less likely to get into trouble as she so often wandered away from the protection of their company.

And how was it her own heart had become so hopelessly involved? It was long since old Antonio, their leader, had had any hold over her. Her beloved husband had rescued her and given her the security she had craved, but now, a lonely widow, somehow it had been planted in the heart of the shrewd trader that she was the one to restore to life this bawling scrap of humanity. Well, Freya, as his men had decided to name her, had certainly been worth the saving, for though he had told Maria little about it, without doubt the story of her rescue had been a miracle.

And you thought she was off your hands now, didn't you? Maria was silently chiding herself. There is no retirement for you. Your family learned to manage well enough without you all these years. They don't seem to need you, but just maybe you are needed here. Yet it is going to take more than you to help her. I think your Spice Maiden is suffering from a broken heart.

She remained resting there quietly, and as a soft wind caressed her, carrying to her again the piping of the goat herd, she was aware of the perfume coming from Freya's herb gardens. Here was fragrance for healing, for romance and pleasure beyond description, and yet it did not seem to be within the reach of the young gardener.

CHAPTER 2
MEMORIES AWAKENING

Next morning Maria was awakened by the gentle song from the labourers in the olive grove further up the hillside. She found a pitcher of water, bread and fruit put ready for her on the balcony of the little cottage Freya had made available for her.

Already the servants of the household were about their daily tasks, a hive of industry, making the most of the cool morning breezes. Still weary from her journey, and unused to having no task awaiting her, she sat quietly, trying to marshal her turbulent thoughts into order.

Why had she come here? Surely the little scrap of life who had been thrust into her arms, giving her the responsibility of whether she would live or die, and who had somehow grown into a graceful gazelle with this very special gift of awareness of various fragrance, could not be in need of her care now she was married to a prosperous land-owner and settled in to her new estate.

And yet, - and yet, she had had this strong conviction that Freya was in need of her old Nona. She had been so very unwell and not in her right mind when they had released her into the care of the Prince, now her husband, and certainly she seemed to be recovered now physically, so how could it be that, so far away, she had felt this deep concern for her child? Could this have arisen out of her own desire to feel of use, for yes, she had been made well aware that she was no longer needed by the family. Her dear old Dad, who had stayed on in the family farm, growing progressively feeble, must have become tired of waiting for her return and had long since breathed his last. She had returned from their last trip to be told the farm was now sold. They showed her the old olive tree under which they had buried him, and her own children were by now grandparents. Yes, the next generation of grandchildren had given her a joyful welcome and yet, there seemed to be no need she could fill. How could there be when she had been away for such long stretches at a time?

Well, she would have to give herself a few days before she could face the journey back to her own village up on the hillside above the harbour, and trust that in the meantime she might find some corner where she could meet a need here on this beautiful island with her Freya. Maria knew well enough she would never have been welcomed among those rugged spice traders if her little one had not proved to be of such importance to them. She knew too that now, as an old woman, she could no longer face a future of constant travel, even if they had wanted her – which they had not.

Having washed her face and broken her fast she set out to wander up to the olive grove to see if she could help with the harvest, but on the way she came upon her own Spice Maiden, her garment tucked around her as she tended her herb garden. She leapt up eagerly to embrace the older woman.

'Oh Nona, Nona, you are really here. I wondered if I had just dreamed it. Oh, how my heart has been crying out for you.'

A tear glistened in her eye. She quickly pushed it away but her laugh came over as harsh and metallic as she struggled to hide her emotions.

'Oh, I guess I have just been feeling homesick, only we have never had much of a place to call home, have we?' At that her tears took over and Maria provided an ample bosom for her to snuggle into.

'Well, yes, I would have been quite content to keep you all to myself and to stay in our little cottage on the farm, but you see, Freya, you have a very special gift. At first it was the myrrh that you were aware of. You ran after anyone with the faintest scent upon them, crying out for your mother. It seems your poor dear mother had a locket of myrrh around her neck when they found her body floating….. Oh, oh, I'm sorry my dear,' for Freya was reacting to this retelling of her story, not with another outburst of tears as she might have expected. No, she seemed to be hunching herself up into that foetal position as she had done before, but this time almost in anger.

'I'm so so sorry,' Maria repeated apologetically.

Freya reached out a hand to reassure her.

'No, no. I have to face it. We have hidden it all away for too long. You are not my grandmother. I am just a poor little waif whose own mother thought nothing of risking my life. What mother would do such a thing – (her hands went to her own womb almost involuntarily) to deliberately set out on a journey so full of risk and adventure with a tiny child in tow. What is it they call it? Infanticide?'

Maria pulled the girl to her feet from where she had been squatting in a vain suggestion of continuing her work among the seedlings, and led her to a sheltered bower.

'You mustn't talk like that my dear. Your bitterness can affect the little one you are carrying. Don't judge your mother. You don't know what forces drove her to be in such a position. Your mother loved you. I am sure of it.'

The girl tried to laugh but it came out as a snort.

'What makes you so sure?'

'Why I am as sure as I am that *I* could never have turned you away or given up on you when Old Aba brought you to me. How you had survived being cared for by those rough men I don't know, but survive you did – and survive you will,' she added, aware of the anguish still in the girl's eyes.

'I would happily have kept you as my own and brought you up to help to care for the flock and spin and weave, and end up by marrying one of our shepherd lads. But no. Once Aba recognised you had this very special gift which could help him as a spice trader you could not be left to this simple life, but neither could you be prized from my heart and so poor old Maria had to leave all her home comforts and trail along with you too. And now, see where it has led.'

At this Freya's anger seemed to melt away but again she was shaking with sobs.

'Oh, my lamb, my lamb. Tell your Nona. What is it?'

Freya drew away, angry with herself for displaying such emotion.

'Oh, I've no idea. I feel all mixed up and confused. I don't know anything about my parents, except that they could not have cared about me. You say that I was always hoping to find my mother, but I have no remembrance of that at all. But there was something else I was seeking.'

'Yes?' Maria queried.

'It was that wonderful fragrance. It was as if I caught whiffs of it along the way. It seemed to be leading me on, coming closer and closer, and then suddenly it was gone, like a fragrant candle snuffed out. It wasn't a memory, but rather as if it were a future hope. I don't know how to describe it.

'I know I should be happy to have a good marriage, - but what is marriage if you are not loved?'

A girl ran from the house to call her and Maria was left, puzzling and pondering. How could such a beautiful and apparently successful young woman, having hope of everything she could desire, seem to have become so hopeless.

Had she been brought here now in some way to help her? But how? What could she do?

CHAPTER 3
DREAMS OF LONG AGO

Maria sank down against the wizened trunk of the olive tree, now denuded of all its fruit. She had been happy enough to be included in the group of young women who, inviting her to join them in the harvest, were joyfully shaking the poor old trees until every last olive had fallen into their outspread cloths.

They had gone off to sit in the shade to rest and eat, and Maria had stayed on, resting quietly, realising she had lost her once youthful vigour.

'I'm like this poor old tree,' she sighed. 'My time of fruitfulness of over. My lovers long ago abandoned me, leaving me their children to nurture. And they, do they ever think of their mother? Though I guess it was I who walked out of their lives. Old Aba is the only one who did not forget me, but only because he had some use for me, thinking I could give this little miracle scrap of humanity a chance of survival.

'That was alright. I was still in the village, my grandchildren still around me. She was growing up as one of my family, until I was foolish enough to let the captain know that she had this special gift. Then, of course, it was when he wanted to take Freya with him on his travels in search of spices that I found she had entwined her heart around mine and there was no way I could allow her to go without her old Nona to care for her.'

Exhausted from her labours with the olive pickers, Maria's head slipped forward onto her chest. She was lulled at first by the motion of the waves, until she was back in this repetitive dream.

'Nona! Oh Nona! Come, let me get you into the shade. How long have you been sitting here?' Maria raised her head, struggling to realise where she was, and allowed her Spice Maiden to lead her to her specially sheltered bower.

'Oh, my dear Nona, you are shaking. You must not try to work like the young women. I know you are not old, but you are not young either, and I still need you.'

'No, no. You do not need me now. You have a husband, and servants to care for you. I was foolish to think you needed me.'

Freya's voice became harsh. 'Servants? They care because we pay them. What kind of care is that? And a husband who is away on his travels all the time. I think he bought me because Aba bragged to him of my gift, but now this is gone he will not want me.'

Maria went to reassure her that this was not so, but Freya drew away and got up to leave, even while Maria was begging her to stay.

'No no, you wait here. I am just going to get you some refreshments.' The older woman watched her go, realising that her walk, her talk, had all changed. She was brittle, almost harsh, so unlike the loving, excitable child for whom life had always seemed to be an adventure. At first it was a search for her mother, following any lead of the perfume of myrrh, but then, when they set out on their travels with the spice merchants, there was something more, always something more until……… Until what? And what was it that had changed her now from hope to a hardness, bitterness even?

Freya was beside her again. She helped her to walk up to the house, having insisted that she have some refreshment and a noon tide siesta, but Maria knew that they needed to talk and that somehow they had to go on this journey of exploration together. Maybe it could be the answer and she would have her Spice Maiden restored to her. Maybe. Well, she could but try.

It was another two days before she felt she had the opportunity. They had been helping the young women in the vineyard until the sun was high in the sky and they had been forced to rest in the shade.

'Since I have come to the island,' Maria began, 'I am having this dream. As I sleep, somehow I think I am on a ship. No, not one of the little fishing vessels that carry us between the islands. It is an old ship, not any ship we have ever sailed on together, and we have been on a few haven't we? Somehow I think it just might be the very same ship that the men told me about, that was wrecked all those years ago when they had sailed out to those islands. And so now I am wondering whether, maybe the dream is not mine but yours.'

Freya stood up to go, expressing impatience, but Maria challenged her.

'Is there some task where you are needed?'

Reluctantly she sat down again. 'What is it you want?'

The older woman gently reached out to stroke the girl's hand.

'Sometimes it is good to awaken memories that have long been sleeping. What say we play a game of recollection? Let's see what sort of a picture we can build up between us. Tell me, what are your earliest memories?'

They sat in silence for a while until Maria became aware of the distant bleat of a goat and then, yes, carried on the wind, a sweet melody from Justus's pipe. The laughter of girls returning to work in the vineyard seemed to awaken Freya from a trance. She shifted, as if thinking they should maybe re-join them, but the older woman restrained her, placing her own hand firmly on Freya's.

'Where have you been?' Maria challenged her. 'What are your memories? 'Can you tell me?'

'You were cooking, Nona. Just like you usually are, but you had a little helper.'

'You?'

'Yes, your busy little helper, with her nose exploring every jar for her favourite spices.'

Maria was still holding Freya's hand and now lifted it to her lips. 'Oh, you were such a joy to me. How thankful I am for the day they brought you to me. Do you remember that day?'

Freya shook her head in wonder. She reclaimed her hand and now shifted her position so that she was gazing into the eyes of her friend.

'I remember the day they arrived.' Maria continued. 'Old Antonio, - Aba we all began to call him now he was grown older. He had long been a trader, travelling the world in search of exotic herbs and spices that he could use in his trading, but from time to time he would come back to his roots, and now, with a helpless child on his hands he told me, 'If she has a chance of living, I knew we must speed our way to bring her to you.'

'He had not doubted but that I would agree. And how could I not? I held out my arms to his pathetic little bundle. You seemed to be almost too weak to cry, but though my breasts were long since shrivelled, my heart was crying out for someone to love, for my youngest had not long got married and her husband had taken her with him to the mainland.'

'But where had he got me? Surely no one would have traded him with a little child?'

'Oh, never, never. No one would have wanted to buy you anyway, you were such a poor little thing. No, he was rambling on about a shipwreck, and something about a miracle, but I never could get much out of him. We'll have to get hold of him and find out the full story.'

Freya sat there in silence for a while. 'I had a mother,' she said, as if awakening from a reverie. Then - 'There was the myrrh'- Both women had spoken, almost in unison.

'Yes, yes.' Maria was getting excited. 'You always recognised the perfume of myrrh, though of course you did not know its name. I happened to mention this to Aba. He did not react at first, but then later he showed me this locket. It was retrieved from the wreck. Silver it was – with some emblem inscribed on it, and it held a sachet of myrrh. I wanted him to give it to you, but he said he wouldn't give it to you, for it was of value and people might even kill you to steal it. Did he give it to you when you left him to be married?'

'No.'

'He should have done. Surely he had not traded it?

'I remember now how, when Antonio visited us, returning from yet another expedition and I had first mentioned your obsession with this particular perfume he had almost shame-facedly produced it from his satchel.

''I had intended to trade with it, but somehow I have never been able to complete the transaction,' he told me.

He showed it to you and let you wear it. It seemed to be of special comfort to you, but then he took it back, promising to guard it safely for you.'

Freya shook her head in wonderment, for a vague memory had been awakened. Somehow just the telling of the story was bringing a measure of comfort.

'It must have reminded you of your mother,' Maria continued.

The two women sat in silence for a while, again the strains of Justus's pipe providing background music for their thoughts.

'I think we need to find Old Antonio.' Maria burst out. 'We know you had a mother. Babies don't just land from the sky, or the sea, come to that. So how did they come to rescue a dear little toddler like you? And how could a loving mother have put her darling child at such risk?'

'Perhaps she wanted to be rid of me?'

Maria was quick to rebuke her charge. 'Never! Never! To want rid of a dear little thing like you. I refuse to believe it. Don't even think such a thing.'

That night Maria dreamed again of the sea, and once again it seemed she was on a ship, a very old ship that creaked and groaned against the battering of the wind and waves.

She did not see her Freya again until mid-morning the following day, and the young woman looked as if she had had her own storm.

'I'm going to get hold of that Old Antonio,' Maria resolved. 'We need to get to the bottom of this mystery, but how?' How indeed? What was the possibility of him ever coming to their remote island? And there was no way she would leave her dear Freya when she was in such evident need of her.

CHAPTER 4
A MESSAGE FROM THE PRINCE

It was a day or two later. The old rooster had wakened them early, warning them not to waste the cool of the morning. Maria wandered into Freya's herb garden and was down on her knees beside her Spice Maiden to join her in planting out some seedlings.

'What are they?' she asked, sniffing. 'Surely these stubby green things should be in your vegetable garden, not here, among your sweet smelling fragrances.'

'Ah, you will see, - once we are at the stage of extracting the oils, these will have a use in creating a base in which to store the perfume. Or so I am told. We will see.'

The sun was rising higher in the heavens and Maria was glad to sit back, stretching out to caress her poor cramped legs. Freya beckoned her to their bower, where one of the servants had already set out refreshment for them. 'Tell me,' she asked. 'What was it made you realise I was good with spices, and how did it happen that Aba wanted us to join his caravan?'

As Maria meditated, a smile curled to Freya's lips. 'If we had stayed in your village I would never have ended up married to my prince.'

Oho, thought the older woman. So he is your prince? Underneath this brittle exterior there is a tender heart towards her husband. But why is he not here enjoying each day with this beautiful wife? But first she had Freya's question to answer.

'You loved to help me when I was cooking. You would run to fetch each jar and to savour its own aroma, before watching me take just a pinch to add to my pot. But then, when we went to the market and women were there each with her own little oven and selling meals to the sailors as they came off the ships, you would squat down nearby, aware of any new fragrance or spice that you had not yet found in my kitchen and so together we were discovering new ingredients.

'And then, once Aba came and realised you were of use to him in discovering new spices in which he could trade..............'

Maria stopped, aware she no longer had her attention. For Freya was on her feet, whipping off her gloves and apron and making for the house.

'Freya, what is it?' Maria called after her retreating form, but there was no hope of an answer from her or anyone else for the whole household was transformed into a hive of industry. Freya was shouting directions here and there as she called her personal maid to help her don her best gown.

Maria was able to catch one of the servants for long enough to question her. 'Why, the ship from the mainland is in and there is a visitor on his way. Justus is not sure if it is the master yet, but we have to be ready.'

Justus? The goat herd? At last Maria was able to piece two and two together. He was not just piping out his joyful tunes for himself and his goats, but was sending messages to those on the estate up in the hills. So that was how she had known I was on my way and came so swiftly to greet me, she thought. Oh my, how slow I have been.

She left the busy workers as they twined boughs of frangipani and myrtle over the veranda, and prepared cooling drinks and other assurances of welcome while she too washed her face and tidied herself. Not that anyone would notice her.

Freya had run to a rise in the hillside but already Justus was piping out another message. Maria watched her shake her head and with drooping shoulders return to sit on the veranda. An elderly steward was sent in her place to welcome their visitor and soon was returning to the house with a distinguished looking gentleman by his side.

The foreign looking gentleman knelt at Freya's feet, taking the hand she proffered him and kissing it with great respect.

'Your husband, the Prince, sends you his deep regret that he has left you for so long,' he began. 'I come bearing a gift from him, and also a letter which explains the gift to you.' He handed a package with some knobs protruding which suggested that it might be a scroll.

'He said, that if you choose, I could read his greeting to you, or, if you prefer, I am instructed to spend some time to teach you to read, so that you can read for yourself his very personal and tender epistle, and you will then also be able to enjoy this wonderful manuscript which he knows will be of great joy to you.

'He wanted to assure you that he wishes to make all speed to return to your arms, but meanwhile he has great longing that his wife may have added the gift of literacy to her many other gifts and charms.'

Freya took her husband's letter into her hands, obviously longing to hear its contents. Could she contain this longing until she was able to acquire a seemingly impossible skill of learning to read? She had never been to school. Surely this was only for the male sex?

Maria watched with bated breath. What would her Freya choose? And if her child's love were great enough to choose the path of a scholar, would there still be any place in her life for her Nona?

CHAPTER 5
MEMORIES UNLOCKED

Old Antonio groaned, his head sinking lower on his chest. Why had he allowed himself to be lured here by old Maria, to have these memories awakened?

He had spotted her, sitting on the harbour wall, as soon as they had sailed into the harbour. There was a time when the sight of her would have sent his heart racing. He could hardly have waited to unload their cargo and then, arms around each other's waists, they would have bounded up the narrow streets to her little cottage on the hillside where she would have had his favourite stew already simmering on a little fire.

Now he had not altogether forgotten his patient wife and the children waiting for him in the town, but he deserved a little spoiling with this temptress, who still seemed to be foot loose and fancy free, though no longer the pretty little Maria, but was now the wrinkled old grandmother who all those years ago had been willing to leave her by now scattered family to care for their Spice Maiden.

Oh yes, he had seen her, and she must have known he was deliberately avoiding her, but still she waited, sitting on the quay side. Oh, how stubborn these women can be, he thought. He sighed once he saw she had gone, only to find she had left a message for him.

'Maria says she has your favourite stew waiting for you.' Oh dear. An old man may no longer be tempted by a woman's body, - certainly not that of an old woman anyway, but Maria's stew? And oh, he hadn't realised how hungry he was.

Maria, having filled his dish yet again with the last scraping from the pot, filled up his tankard, then pulled up her chair so that she was looking him in the eye.

'And you haven't even asked about our lassie. You have a guilty conscious, haven't you? Oh Aba. Shame on you. As soon as my back is turned I find you have sold her off for a bride price.'

'Now, now Maria. What could I have done? She seemed to have lost her desire, or gift was it, of searching out new perfumes and spices and it was as though she had fallen into a terrible pit of depression. We were fearing even for her life.'

Maria nodded. 'Not just her, I think. There was darkness and fear and depression all around us, and we all wanted to get away.

'Do you remember how, we were coming from Damascus and we met up with these other Greeks?' she added. 'They were on their way to Jerusalem for the feast? It was they who had told us about the wonderful fragrances the Jews used in their worship.....'

'Yes, yes,' the captain interrupted, 'but then when we got there, Freya was more interested in meeting this man, - Jesus, remember? – than these fragrant offerings. And one of them said he had a friend Philip who was one of Jesus' followers, and he was sure he would arrange it for us all. So we waited, but it didn't work out did it? And then it wasn't just our Freya. I know she seemed to be out of her mind, but there was to be a terrible gloom and foreboding over the whole city and so I decided we had better get away as soon as we could and maybe make for Lebanon.'

Maria was still facing him, looking him straight in the eye. 'Yes,' she challenged? He hadn't yet answered her question. Antonio groaned. 'Well, you will remember, I had met the Prince before – I think the first time was in Persia, and then later in Cathay. He had shown interest in our Freya and then, there he was, and still ready with his offer to marry her.

'It was such a provision that it was he who had invited us to bring our Freya to his encampment to be cared for, for she was so ill. And his offer again now of marriage seemed like a good idea, for you knew you were getting too old to continue travelling around with her, and we needed to get her out of that terrible place where all seemed doom and gloom. And then, when you were called away, first to find your friend, and then helping someone in labour was it? I thought I had best complete the transaction without your reproaches....'

'Truly,' Maria interrupted, 'but have you any idea of how she is *now*? You have prospered through her gifts all these years and yet where is your sense of responsibility? What about how she is doing now?'

Spluttering over his wine, poor old Antonio tried to justify himself, but the old woman silenced him. 'No, you listen and *I* will tell you what I know. When you first brought that little bundle of life to me, I loved her. And when you returned and discovered her gift and wanted to take her with you on your journeys it was love that dragged me all those miles and through all those adventures, and yes, you may have discarded her and thought you were finished with her, but my love would not let her go.'

'So you *did* find a ship to take you to their Isle of Fair Winds, once we had learned of its name?'

He was alert now, wanting to know more.

'Oh yes, I did indeed. She is a grand lady now, with a wonderful estate, and gardens and groves. And while her prince is away, gallivanting around the world, he is expecting her to develop some exotic perfume which will bring him yet more riches.

'Oh yes, Aba….. You may well smirk, thinking you have done well for her, but listen. Our little lassie is with child. Her husband is away, she knows not where, and she is concerned that this child will be born to one who was unloved and unwanted and so can never make a good mother.'

The old spice trader tipped up his tankard to drain the last dregs, wiped his mouth and then his eyes.

'How can she think that?' he demanded. 'Her parents were wealthy, important people. I'm sure they loved her very much.'

'Oh yes?' Maria was waiting for more. 'And how do we know that? Come, come,' she urged, impatiently. 'You need to tell me what you know, for her mind must be set at rest if that child is to be brought forth safely.

'Do you know Freya has been having a persistent dream about this old ship? Then I began to have these dreams too, only whereas her dreams were of being gently rocked by the waves, my dreams were terrible, - of crashing and dashing – of terror and disaster.'

They both sat in silence while the shadows lengthened and at last she got up to find a taper and using the glow of the fire, lit her oil lamp and set it on its stand. It was then the old man began to tell his version of that tragic story.

CHAPTER 6
TREASURE WRAPPED IN SEAWEED

It was a while before old Antonio raised his head and began to speak, but his voice was low and Maria was straining forward to catch his words.

'It was when we were following the old Silk Road that we heard tell of these islands where an exotic fruit grew which was being introduced in the spice trade. Sensing the possibility of rich pickings, I found out more, and once we had reached a port I set out to look for a ship willing to turn from its usual route to see if we could find this particular island.

'The lad in the crow's nest has spied land in the distance, but then it seems as if the elements are determined to protect its discovery from invaders.' Maria glances at the old man, and can see that memory has carried him back so that once again he is standing in the bows of the ship. 'An eerie light is dimming the sun and now the wind is whipping the seas into a frenzy.' His voice gets stronger as he continues.

'The captain orders the sails furled and we drop anchor. Aye, he's hoping we can ride out this storm that is threatening. All but the crew have been ordered below decks. Yes, I have to obey, but it isn't long before I creep up again, for if this is to be our last adventure I do not want to spend it in darkness. We are all beginning to wonder if this one is to prove one too many.'

There was a long pause, and Maria gave him a shake, holding out his tankard, freshly filled. 'Come on, Aba. We know you survived, so don't leave me in suspense. What about Freya?'

He emptied his tankard and then, as if making a supreme effort, continued, but again his voice is sinking to a whisper. He seems to be back in that horrific situation.

'At last we are all called up to the deck. The light is still dim, but the seas much calmer now though the wind still high. Instead of using sail the men are rowing cautiously towards land. We begin to see – a piece of broken spar; - sail cloth ripped to shreds. And then' – he pauses and shudders, living it all again. 'We see – yes, a body, and then another. I notice the remains of a tattered garment, but there is gold thread in the cloth. We are all shocked; crying out at the horror of it.'

Maria puts her arm around the old man and helps him to mop his face.

'Shall we leave the story for another day?' she suggests, but reluctantly, for who knew what a day might bring? She was relieved when, after another draught from his tankard, he stood up, tottered to the door and breathed in the warm night air, doubtless relieved himself, then sat again to continue.

'This ship must have been ahead of us in this quest for riches. In our greed we would have wished to have been ahead of them, but we well knew now that this then might well have been our fate. But even in our shock and thankfulness that we were alive, greed was still alive and well too, and the men, yes, us too, were grabbing for anything that was worth saving, for these were all dead bodies.'

'But what about our Freya?' Maria blurted out. Aba, now definitely back in the present, shook an angry finger at her. 'Don't interrupt Woman, or you'll hear no more.'

Silence. Maria dare not try to coax him again. At last he resumed, but again now as if he was speaking from far away.

''Aba! Come! Come!' We all ran then, but the captain shouted at us lest the ship capsize with us all to one side, and then ordered the lowering of the life boat. I made sure I was in it. There was a mass of seaweed bobbing gently as the waves were breaking on the shore.

''What is it?' I asked Toma, the man who had first cried out to me.

''Aba, I saw movement. I swear there is life there.' He stepped out of the boat now, for we were nearing land and gently lifted up the bundle, pulling back the weeds to reveal the form of a little child and waded with her to the shore.'

'Our Freya,' Maria murmured.

'Yes, our Freya.' Antonio responded, wrapped again in awe and wonder as on that day, so long ago. 'It was as if the seaweed had been sent to protect her, for air must have been trapped within this nest so that she had been kept alive.'

The two sat in silence for a long time until the lamp was burning dim and the fire again just a glow.

'You can see how Freya feels she was unloved. How could her parents have put her life too at risk in their mad search for riches?' Maria began to weep.

'Now, stop ya blubbering woman,' Antonio spoke roughly to hide his own emotion. 'I'll wish I had not told you, if all you're going to do is weep.'

'Oh Aba,' she pleaded, 'don't scold me. I had thought that somehow there might be something in the telling that could have been of some comfort to our lovely Freya, to help her to carry her own child safely.'

The fire had almost given up its last glow as the two old people sat either side of its embers, when suddenly Maria stirred. She was on her feet now.

'Come on, old man. You have not told me everything, have you?' Her voice was imperious, demanding.

He spluttered as he again sought refuge in this drink. 'What do you mean, woman?'

'You did find out something about her parents. And what about the ship? Come on now, rake through your memories, while I start to rake through these embers.'

Antonio tottered outside to find some sticks to help kindle the blaze, then sat again to find Maria had not given up on her accusation.

'What do you mean?' He was trying to put on a look of injured innocence, but she would have none of it.

CHAPTER 7
ANTONIO IN TROUBLE

Dawn had long broken when the old man awoke, still in his seat in Maria's cottage.

'Oh, dear, what a welcome I'll get from the wife,' he complained. 'Why did you not drive me home long ago? You always used to.'

'And so I would have done if you had told me all you knew. I've got to return to our Lassie, and I am not going without some glimmer of hope that we are able to trace her parents.

'I would never have left her, for she seemed to cling to me, but this stranger arrived with messages from her husband and all else was put on hold as she began her lessons in learning how to read. And when I heard that there was a ship in port that would bring me back to my own place I knew I must come and find you as you were the only one who could tell us all that is known of our Freya's beginnings.

'So here I am, and I am not leaving, nor are you come to that, until you have told me all you know.'

'So what makes you think I have more to tell?' the old man grumbled.

'While you have been snoring, I have been sitting here, searching through the memories that are tumbling around in my head.

'Come to think of it, there is a whole story to be told as to how you ended up bringing this little child to *me*. You could soon enough have found a wet nurse even on those islands, or in any of the lands where you set foot on the long journey back to this, our homeland. Somebody would have given you good money for a golden haired lassie as she was.'

The old man began to cough and splutter again as he tried to concoct a likely story to explain the unexplainable, but Maria's imagination worked quicker than his. She sat back now on her haunches as she looked up from tending the fire.

'You didn't know anything of her gift with the fragrances then, and yet you knew she was somehow of worth, of value to you! Yes, yes, don't try to deny it. I am getting to the bottom of it now, aren't I?'

The old spice trader could not look her in the eye. She allowed him to mutter complaints into his beard before she pressed him any further. At last he took up his tale.

'Aye, you are right, old woman. I knew the locket holding her sachet of myrrh was of great value, and maybe even gave the secret of her ancestry. That was why I would not sell her to just anyone, and when at last we took a vessel that brought us homeward, and I realised that we were just a stone's throw from your cottage, I knew I should see if I could persuade you to take on the care of the little one. After all, you had never driven me away before, and if she was with you I knew I need not lose track of her.'

'Oh, and what a treasure you brought me.' Maria sighed, back in her chair and rocking gently, as if reliving the joy the little child had brought into her life. 'But ' -   She leaned forward, shaking old Aba's arm. 'I am remembering now our little one, running after people, always searching for her Mamma, and eventually realising it was the perfume of myrrh that was awakening something within her...'

A guilty look spread over his wizened face. 'Oh, ah, aye.' He nodded, recognising whence this was leading.

'And you told me how you had found this locket of myrrh that her mother had been wearing around her neck?'

'Yes.' Mariah was accusing now. 'And you took out the cluster of myrrh and gave it to her, but it wouldn't have survived the sea water if it had not been in some special locket, now would it?' She held him in the spotlight of her glare.

'Come! Come, Aba. You didn't give her all you had found, did you?'

'Of course I didn't. It would have been putting the child in danger to let her have the care of something of such value. I was keeping it for her.'

'So? Where is it? You have no right to keep it now she is married and has someone to protect her. Surely you should have given it to her?'

'Yes, yes. Of course.' But the old man was still wriggling under Maria's scrutiny.

'Then does it give any clue?' she persisted.

'Not to me it didn't, but I knew it was valuable, and I kept it among my treasures in case the need arose for us to barter it. And that is what I did.

'Hush now woman,' he warned as Maria, red with indignation, opened her mouth to continue her accusations. 'I gave it to her prince by way of a bride price and he seemed more than satisfied.'

Lost for words, the old woman rose, having coaxed the fire into life and began to prepare some porridge, knowing well that poor Antonio was not likely to be fed by a neglected wife. Warmed and fed, the questioning continued.

'Where did you produce him from, anyway? It seems strange to me how quickly it all happened, and behind my back too,' she added, reaching out a bony finger to give him a poke. 'I have never dared to ask our Freya, last it bring on again the terrible brain sickness that attacked her when we were in the city of Jerusalem.'

'Keep your fingers to yourself, and I'll tell you. You were so angry at the time that you never gave me a chance to explain.'

He made as to rise, as if he needed to go outside on some excuse or other but she angrily pushed him back into his seat. He had better come up with the truth before he would find any comfort.

'Yes, yes,' he mustered testily and then, knowing she would brook no more delays, he began yet another story in this devious unravelling.

'Our paths had crossed a few times in our travels, and he had shown interest in our Spice Maiden, but as we were now in lieu of parents to her, there was no way I would sell her as a child bride. We moved on then, trying to keep away from him.'

'Yes, Maria, agreed, 'and we tried to disguise her as a lad, so that we would not have any other offers of marriage.'

'Yes,' Antonio confirmed, not welcoming the interruption, 'But, well, you know how there seemed to be some special fragrance that was always leading her on?'

Maria was nodding assent, urging him to continue. 'And then, when we got in with this party of Greeks making their way to Jerusalem for their special feast..'

'Yes, and we met this man who said he knew Philip, who was a friend of this Jesus, and could arrange for us to meet him and now Freya was convinced that she was nearing the source of this fragrance…'

Antonio was allowed to butt in here; 'but Philip came back to say this Jesus couldn't, or was it wouldn't meet with us, and at this she seemed to be plunged into a terrible darkness.

'It was as if her depression was a precursor to the darkness that was creeping over the whole of the city. You went off to try to fetch your friends and had not yet returned, and I felt I had to get her away from this cursed place. The Prince came to me at this time and renewed his offer, and I felt it was a wonderful provision for our spice maiden, but what would he ask by way of a bride price?'

'You could well have afforded a good one,' Mariah chided.

The old man spluttered. 'What? To give away our Spice Maiden, our best asset in seeking out spices?' he argued. 'Anyway, he was more than content to take her locket, and he promised he would hold it in trust for his bride, and yes,' he conceded, 'he did make it worth my while.'

Their conversation was about ended when some youths arrived to escort their father home, while Maria ran to her larder to pile a basket with sweet meats as a gift for his neglected wife.

Once they were gone, Mariah collapsed onto a chair in the sun, her eye lids drooping, and her mind a jumble of questions as to the worth of a bundle of myrrh which seemed to have miraculously been preserved in a silver locket through that disastrous storm and shipwreck.

She knew they were no further on in their dreaming, but after a long sleep she awakened, knowing she must get back to her Freya.

CHAPTER 8
TRAIL OF MEMORIES

Maria had heard Justus, the goat herd, piping his spritely tune, realising by now that he was announcing that a visitor was approaching, but she continued to plod her way upward until she reached the grateful shade of the parklands that were part of Freya's estate. It was only then that she caught a glimpse of her beloved Spice Maiden. She had come out to stand on the vine covered veranda to await her. Gracefully curved now and no longer able to trip lightly, there was a bloom on her cheeks and a glow of wellbeing about her, and she welcomed her dear Maria with delight.

'Yes,' she assured her, she had heard the boy's piped announcement, 'but this is my lesson time. Oh Maria, I used to dread this hour with my teacher. You see, my husband, Prince Hermas had sent him with a letter to me, but he was not to read it to me. He was to teach me to read so that I could read it for myself.' Maria nodded. She had known that far.

'At first I dreaded his lessons. I was convinced that it was not possible for a village girl like me to learn to read.'

Maria snorted. 'Village girl, indeed! Just because you've been brought up by a villager does not make *you* a village girl. You are a princess, and you certainly have the gifting of royalty.'

Freya reached over to press her finger to Maria's lips. 'Let me finish my story,' she pleaded.

'I persevered, plodding on with reciting the letters, and then, like the sun rising after a dark night, I found that the letters were joined up to make words I understood.

'Then at last Abba Beni gave me the letter from the Prince, - my husband,' she added in a whisper, as if expressing some wonderful truth.

'Oh Maria.' She stopped to embrace herself, unable to express in words the joy even now it meant to her.

'And at the end of his letter he told me he had purchased an ancient manuscript which he had given into Beni's care, and that he could help me to read it.

'Oh Maria. It is the most beautiful story, of a simple village girl, but I think she must have been a spice maiden too. She loved to be out in the fields and gardens and the story is full of references to some of the spices that we used to find in our travels. But it is a love story, Maria, and I think he sent it to me because it is like *our* story. Her prince would come and visit her, but she never knew when he would come. That is like us. My prince promises me he has not forgotten me, and he assures me he will come soon.

'The goat herd is practising a special melody as soon as he sees a royal party approaching.'

Her hand went to her mouth. 'What is it?' Maria asked. 'Are you in pain?'

Freya was anxious to reassure her. 'No, I was thinking about the book I am reading. Her prince came at times in disguise, so maybe Justus will not recognise our Prince. I had better be ready, even if I get no advance announcement.'

Servants came out then to bring a bowl of fruit, with cheese and bread, for her to share with her visitor, and then Maria was more than ready for a sleep, though she made Freya her excuse.

The servants had taken it for granted that the elderly woman would be staying and she found her little cot all ready for her. Both she and Freya were happy to sleep through the heat of the afternoon, looking forward to a quiet evening when they would recline in hammocks on the veranda as the day faded into the purple hush of evening, their murmured conversation mingling with the chatter of the cicadas and the shrill piping of the bats.

Maria recounted her story of that long evening when she had been seeking to wring out of old Antonio his memories of the shipwreck, but when it seemed to be disturbing long buried memories of the little child wrenched from her mother's arms by the tempest, she realised she needed gently to steer their conversation in another direction.

'Tell me, Little One,' (she still used that term of affection by which she had called the toddler who had been given into her care) 'Do you remember how we met those travellers who were going to Jerusalem for the Jews special feast?'

Freya swung her legs to the ground, and moved into an upright seat. She was animated, a sparkle in her eyes. 'Oh, yes. Yes.'

'What was it that caused you such excitement? Can you remember?'

She was like a fire that had had a flame coaxed from its embers but then it had died away again. Freya slipped back onto her couch, her animation gone.

At last Maria dared to bring up the subject again. 'So what happened? You were all excited, like that merchant who was seeking the finest pearl in the land, and knew that at last he would triumph after a life time of searching.'

'Yes, yes – just like that.' She leant her head against the cushions. Maria heard the quiet step of a servant come to light the lamps, but she motioned to her not to disturb them. There was a distant bleat from the goats in the village, but these women were cocooned in the silence of their own thoughts. At last Freya began what was to be a long story, of a search, not of a pearl, but of a perfume that would surpass the beauty of any fragrance as yet known to man.

'Do you remember?' Freya began. 'The time we had travelled far to the east. You made me dress up as a boy. You said it would be safer, and you allowed me to go to the market place.' Maria wanted to interrupt as she remembered that she had never allowed her to go unless a couple of the older lads were sent to keep an eye on her, but she wisely allowed Freya to continue. She didn't want to spoil her retelling of the story.

'I squatted down beside a lad who was trading saffron. But it was not just the perfume of the saffron that I smelt, though I didn't realise that at the time. Maybe it had come from his head covering. Anyway, he promised to take us to where the saffron grew. That was the first time ever I caught this fragrance. Oh, it was wonderful.

'And you remember, Maria, how they took us far out in the countryside and found fields of the saffron, but then, on the way back it was as if this other, more wonderful fragrance was calling me, and how in the end it led me to the Wise One.' Oh yes, Maria remembered so well, her anxiety over her Spice Maiden, and where this would all lead her.

Freya continued with her story, the story the old man, the Wise One had told her, that day so long ago now, of the star that had foretold the birth of a heavenly King, of their preparation of gifts for such a Holy One and of their long and dangerous journey until at last they found him 'One of our men came to sit with us, to help me understand what the boy was saying. He told us that his father's master was a very wise man, and he knew all about the stars, and how the stars had been telling him that a very special king had been born, and so he and some of his friends, - they were wise ones too, were going to find this king and so they needed very special gifts to take to give to him.'

Maria knew the story so well, remembering her own anxiety when she was not allowed to follow her maiden and the long hours of waiting and wondering, but she was not going to interrupt Freya, for she realised it was she who needed to remember. Somehow she had to piece all these adventures together to make sense of the whole.

'Yes, go on,' she affirmed.

So Freya continued with her version of her meeting in that strange house, and hearing from his own lips the story of the Wise One and how, with his friends they had prepared their gifts and made this awesome journey to find this one who was indeed the promised King; of how they had worshipped him, and somehow carried his fragrance back with them.

Maria did interrupt now.

'I do believe it was after that meeting that you had this special awareness of fragrances and flavours too. But come on, you are supposed to be telling me what happened in Jerusalem,' but Freya did not seem to hear. Maria knew the story well enough but realised there was therapy in them going over the story together.

When eventually Freya took up her account, she was still far from Jerusalem.

'I smelled it again when we were in Egypt.' Maria smiled, as she continued her account, and they laughed and wept together as they reminisced over their meeting with the woman who had taken in the Holy Family and yes, the fragrance that still lingered there on the shores of the River Nile.

Maria waited for Freya to continue. 'Was it the same ..? 'Yes,' she affirmed, 'the same as when we were travelling through the Eastern lands and met with the Wise One.'

'So, were you ever aware of it again?'

Freya seemed lost in her thought for a while and Maria plucked at the grapes that were growing around her. She knew it was important to be patient. But she wanted to know about their time in Jerusalem. She felt she must help to stir their memories.

'Do you remember how we were following the King's Highway and we met the party on their way to the great feast in Jerusalem, and they told us about the amazing fragrances of the incense the Jews offer to their God in the great Temple? Aba determined that we would go there to find the secret of the spices and perfumes they use, and maybe do some trading.'

Freya joined in then. 'Now I remember. It was when we were nearing Jerusalem that Aba told you to take me into this village to ask for lodging for the night, for the crowds were growing and they were having to settle down wherever they could find space to make a camp. He was grumbling that it wasn't suitable for a young girl to have come on such a journey, but we knew it was because I could search out for fresh perfumes and spices that he had always wants us to come along. And of course he was worried because he realised it was getting too much for you, my Nona.'

'Anyway, off we walked in the direction he pointed out until we came to this sleepy little village.'

'I remember now.' Maria joined in. 'I suggested we sit by the well and see if anyone would offer hospitality.'

'But then I was aware of it – the same fragrance.'

'And you then like a hound on the hunt. Dragging me along with my poor weary feet, until we stopped outside a courtyard where all I could smell was the aroma of the evening meal they were cooking.

'They gave us such a welcome, and we shared this delicious stew.'

'Yes, I know, it was a delicious stew, but it was not this that had attracted me. A child came to the gate and, seeing us, called to her grandmother, and it wasn't long before we were invited in and seated around their table and sharing their supper. We talked about their special feast, Passover, they called it, and they told us that tomorrow they intended to go into the city, but all the time I was aware of the fragrance. Somehow I was beginning to realise that it was for this that I had been spared and rescued after the terrible storm and shipwreck, for this we had come to share a meal with this family, but before I knew how to find an answer to the searching of my heart, the matron of the family called us and directed us to the shade of the fig tree. 'You go and sit there and talk to my mother while we prepare you sleeping accommodation. She has a story she would love to share with you.'

Once again Maria sat back while her Freya recounted the wonderful story the woman's daughter had told them, of the terrible suffering of the residents of their little town of Bethlehem, of the wonderful birth of this special family, but the awful repercussions when Herod's men came in search of this Child. Failing to find him, they had rampaged through the town and how her baby brother had been snatched from her mother and slaughtered in front of her eyes and she had lost her mind with the grief – until –

Like the family who had told them the story, Freya seemed silenced by the joy of their memories, and eventually Maria came to her aid.

'It was Jesus, wasn't it?' she gently prompted.

'Yes, she told us how she was sitting with the children. She had the baby on her knee when he came and held out his arms for her to place the baby in them.'

And then it was as if all the memories that had been hidden deep away were brought to the surface and Freya began to weep as she had not been able to weep before, even while Maria was helping her in the telling.

'Yes, yes. And he said to her, "Your baby died so that I could be saved." Freya paused for some moments, then spoke as if from far away.

'But he said something else too. Remember, Maria? Something about, I am soon to die, that your little ones may yet be restored to you? Oh, oh Maria – always hope and yet always this terrible gloom.'

Maria did not know how to answer. They sat in silence for a while.

Again the servant came in to light the lamps, but Maria signalled to her that her mistress was ready to rest.

'Go to your bed now, my little Spice Maiden,' she whispered as she dried Freya's tears, 'I've a feeling there is going to be a happy ending for your story too. Sleep well and pleasant dreams.'

CHAPTER 9
PRISCA'S HELP WITH THE STORY TELLING

It was several days before Freya was able to continue her story. Maria had wakened, looking forward to hearing the next episode through the eyes of her Spice Maiden, but she had to be patient, for the young mother to be had risen early, bursting with energy.

'Oh, madam, the mistress is in her garden. She says there is work to be done, in case the Prince arrives unexpectedly.'

Maria wished she might feel some of Freya's energy. Though she had offered to help with transplanting some of the precious plants, she had been grateful not to have her offer accepted. She had pleaded in vain for the young woman to come into the shade to rest, so all she could do was sit there under the shade of the pomegranate trees, watching, and occasionally renewing her plea.

After three days labouring in her herb garden, some sudden pains had driven Freya back to the shade on the veranda. Dared Maria lead her back to their story at this time?

'We met Marcos, didn't we? Do you remember?'

'Of course I remember. We had linked up with those Greeks while we were travelling.' Maria nodded her affirmation. Yes, she remembered well.

'They had been going up to Jerusalem for their special feast. It was when they invited us to sit and share a meal with them that the conversation had turned to this preacher, Jesus. How my ears had pricked up at that name.'

Again she waited for her Nona's nod of confirmation, and went on.

'Then one of them told us about a friend of his, Philip. He was one of Jesus' disciples, and they would all surely be coming to Jerusalem for the feast so he had a very good chance of being able to find him once they had reached the outskirts of the city. He felt sure that Philip would be able to arrange for us to meet up with his master, Jesus.'

'Oh yes, but what happened? Did we meet up with them again?' Maria remembered well enough, but Freya seemed to have sunk back into her memories, and she wanted to encourage her to continue to retell their story. Might it help?

'Why yes, Maria, don't you remember? We did at last meet Philip and he said yes, he would ask Jesus, and he was sure that he would want to meet with them.'

'And? – she looked to Maria to help her continue the story, but Maria was hesitant, unwilling to refer to her child's terrible breakdown. At last she continued.

'You have forgotten. It was at that time that Aba sent me to go and fetch Naomi from their village to come and help. But then I was called away to help this woman in distress, and when I came back you had gone. Aba – all of you. Oh, what a time of it I had, searching for you, for the whole of Jerusalem seemed to be in turmoil at that time. There was talk of earthquakes and a terrible darkness, - and there were rumours that this wonderful Jesus had been arrested. Oh, the stories that were being passed around.'

'No, no, but before that.' But just as Maria had thought that at last she might find out the missing link she was seeking, Prisca had come to insist that it was time for Freya to have some lunch. She had planned a routine of rest and then time with a masseur who had arrived, bringing his own fragrant oils to use as part of his ministry.

Poor Maria sighed. Would she never get to solve this mystery? She wandered out into the olive grove finding a quiet bench where she rested her own weary bones and realising that she too was in need of rest.

A servant girl came out with the usual platter of fruit and goats cheese. 'Prisca asked me to bring you this,' she explained. As she indulged in the succulent grapes and mangoes she began to wonder about Prisca, who seemed to be there to serve everyone and yet was so much more than a servant.

A motherly figure, she obviously was not one of the locals as many of the servants were. Who was she? And how did she have this feeling that somehow she might have seen her before. Was it in a dream? How could that be?

An hour or two had passed when Maria opened her eyes to find it was Prisca herself had come to find her and call her to see if she wanted to help them in preparing the evening meal.

She began to apologise, but Prisca insisted that Maria's one responsibility was to her adopted child, her Spice Maiden. 'It is just that we all enjoy your company, and we know you love to have something to occupy your hands.'

As they walked back to the mansion, arm in arm, Maria's questionings were answered.

'No, no, I was brought up on the mainland, - my parents were servants to the king, and I grew up as one of the household. When my own little son died of a fever, I became more and more involved in the care of the little prince and grew to love him as if he were my own flesh and blood.

'When he was grown he would be away on his travels, sometimes acting as an ambassador on behalf of his father but he had his own interests too, often bringing back plants and saplings and strange spices.'

'So, how did he come to live here, on this island and to make his home here?'

'Why, it was gifted to him by his Father, on condition that he took a bride and settled down. The King had many suggestions, but our Prince insisted that he would only marry one of his own choice.

"Let me go and prepare my inheritance," he pleaded, "and I will go and seek and bring her back myself."

'It was the King who called us, together with some of the younger servants, to accompany his son as he set out. Who knew where we were going?

'The Prince had confided in my husband one evening as they lingered over our meal. It was only later, when all these events occurred so unexpectedly in Jerusalem, that Benin shared it with me.

'It seemed the King, his father, had a choice of suitable brides lined up for him, but the Prince had insisted that he would only marry according to the desire of his own heart, and he insisted too that he knew who it was. He had told Benin,

''I was seeking out fragrant trees, and herbs for my island estate where I was planning to live, for my father had promised it to me. I found myself following the route of the spice traders. We were in a market in this great city in Persia, and as I mingled among the people, the sellers were seeking to tempt us and the traders bartering when I saw this young lad come up to this older man who seemed to be their leader and call him to follow him to where there was a display of something – saffron I think it might have been, but I was more interested in this lad – as I thought, until somehow I became aware that this was no lad, but a beautiful maiden, and there was a special fragrance about her.

''I tried to approach her, but soon found that she was well protected by this group of traders, but it was plain too that she was well loved and in no way an unwilling slave."

Prisca broke into her narrative to look at Maria, who was listening so intently. 'You would have been there, wouldn't you, hovering in the background?'

'I must have been, for we had tried to disguise her as a lad in order to protect her, and if I feared of any unwanted interest I would make sure that I alerted Aba, our leader. And yes, I do have a vague recollection of a young man, obviously of some distinction, though he was wrapped in the robe of a common man, seeking out Aba.'

'Well, our Prince had offered a bride price to your leader, but he insisted she was far too young, but maybe if he approached him in two or three years from then he might reconsider. But it seems he lost touch with you all.'

'Well, yes, we were all so protective of our Spice Maiden, and Aba made sure that we broke camp and hopefully had left no trace.'

'Indeed,' Prisca continued, 'for he had searched far and wide after that, but all in vain. But now his Father, the King, was insisting that he made a marriage by the time Easter had come. Prince Hermas consulted some wise men, and they advised him to make for Jerusalem, where people came from all over the world to attend the special festival of Passover. They knew it was a particularly special festival of the Jewish people, but many others who were searching after the true god would gather too. Why not spice traders among them?

'So it was on the strength of this that we set out.'

'And you, the Prince's nurse maid, were among them?'

Maria was excited. Was she at last going to be able to fit together these missing pieces in her story?

But just then there was a call from the house.

CHAPTER 10
ARRIVAL OF ROYALTY

Since Maria had become aware of her own need to face up to what it was had managed to separate her from her Spice Maiden, she felt she was ready now to understand what had really happened in those dark hours in Jerusalem. She awoke, thinking she was nearing the mystery being resolved, and she would at last hear what it was that had happened in Jerusalem that had changed her whole situation as well as her relationship with her Freya! But it seemed it was not to be, for there was no pitcher of water or tray of breakfast set outside her door. No, she must go in search of these things for herself, otherwise she would go unwashed and hungry. The midwife had been called and the whole of the household was in a state of anxiety.

Oh, dear. Maria longed to go to help her Spice Maiden through this prolonged ordeal. If only the Prince had returned in time, as he had promised.

It was not until the small hours of the next morning that a lusty boy had announced his arrival. It wasn't long before the mother insisted that Maria be called to welcome this child who was not only a grandson of the great King himself, yes, but also in a way, hers too, though she was well aware she had only been a foster mother. What a joy it was to hold this precious gift in her arms. But oh, where was his father, and when would he come?

It was not many days before Freya was recovering her strength, and between the hours she was nursing her child she was concerned to return to her garden, so full of aromatic plants. Then, at last, she heard Justus piping the news she had so longed for. Oh, such a scurrying and hurrying and musicians running down the hillside to welcome the grand entourage of the Prince.

When everything and everyone one was in place for the grand reception, where was the beautiful Princess Freya with the as yet unnamed infant prince, to welcome his father? And come to that, where *was* the Prince Hermas?

Maria and Prisca, were seated, unperturbed, under the pomegranate trees, laughing quietly, for with Maria's knowledge of her Spice Maiden, and Prisca of her Prince, they were not at all surprised that the prince had slipped in quietly and unrecognised, through the back entrance so that at last they were able to have the gentle awakening of love that was so much needed. And the Prince had no intention of rushing this time when at last he was alone with his Spice Maiden and the bonny boy she had born him.

Gently he sat, his arm around mother and child, quietly caressing Freya's cheek, and now and then bending forward to plant a kiss, first on his wife and then on the sleeping prince.

Eventually they made their appearance, a complete family, on the veranda, where the musicians and servants of importance had the opportunity to make their well-rehearsed speeches.

Maria and Prisca knew they would not be needed until the evening when there would be a grand banquet, so after their much needed siesta, they found a shady bower among the olive trees. At last they could continue their task of piecing together the mystery of what had happened, that Easter time in Jerusalem; that time of tragedy that had led on to this time of joy and romance here in the uplands of this beautiful island, part of the kingdom of Grecia, in the lands of the Great Sea.

'I still have anxiety disturbing my breast as I think of those dark days as we drew near to Jerusalem,' Maria began. 'I think we were all weary from our many journeys. I know I certainly was looking forward to returning to my little cottage overlooking the harbour, and wondering how long I could continue to act as shepherd to our Spice Maiden. I confess I had thought of speaking to Aba about finding her a husband, though part of me could not bear the thought of being parted from her.'

'But how was it you were not there with her when she was taken so ill as she was?' Prisca urged her to get on with the story.

'Ah yes.' Maria paused. 'I still wonder about that. How foolish I was, - and and...' Again she paused. Prisca poured her some wine that had been left for them. That seemed to revive her.

'I was so anxious about Freya, for it was obvious she was very ill. I think Aba had suggested I try to find the friends who had shown us hospitality in their village, but their place was empty. And then something else happened to delay me. Oh, yes. I remember now. One of the Greeks we had met at Petra, and with whom we had been travelling, had found this girl who had fallen and gashed her head. He ran up to me and begged me to come and help to bandage the wound and then she went into labour. People were surging around everywhere and I couldn't leave this young girl, but it was as if the whole of the city was in upheaval. Oh Prisca, it was terrible, terrible.' She clung to her friend as if she were again in the midst of that chaotic situation. Eventually she continued her story.

When I eventually got back, I'm sure people thought I was a mad woman as I rushed to and fro seeking for Freya, or indeed for any of our party. But it seemed everyone was in the same state. We didn't know if it was night or day. There was this terrible darkness, as if a great thick blanket had been thrown over our eyes – and.., and I even heard people saying they had seen dead people who were walking about the city. Oh, it was scary.'

Again Maria clung to her friend for reassurance, until she could continue. 'But you got back to your people,' Prisca gently prompted her. Maria nodded. 'Yes, I found some of the others, and gradually found more of our party, and then at last Ben found me and led me back to Aba. I remember, he groaned when he saw me, for I was in such a state. 'Oh no, not you too?' he said.

"What do you mean?" I asked him. Then I demanded, "Where is she?"

'I remember he made them sit me down and give me something strong to drink before he attempted to tell me, but it was a while before I could make head nor tale of his story.

"It was all to do with meeting that Philip," Aba began to tell me. 'Remember he had promised he would make it possible for us to meet with this Jesus everyone is on about, and especially our Freya?'

'I did remember. She had been so sure that he would prove to be the source of this special perfume of which she has been so aware through the years, as we have travelled from place to place. It began when we were following the Spice Road through the kingdom of Persia. We first discovered saffron growing there, but that was forgotten because she recognised something like no other perfume and that is how we heard of the magii, the wise men who had studied the stars and went to the land of Judah because they had seen in the stars that a king had been born.'

'Yes, yes,' I persisted, 'and then, later on, we went to Egypt, and there it was again, and now we had actually met a woman who had not only met this Jesus, but he had healed her – and then Philip told us that he would arrange for us to meet this Jesus…

'But come on, Aba. Where is our Spice Maiden now?' I wanted to reach down his throat to drag it out of him, for I could see he was afraid to tell me. He tried to ply me with more wine, but I would not let him fob me off. I wanted to get hold of him and shake him.

'Poor old Aba. He begged me to let him collect his wits and tell me. It seems there was so much chaos and confusion, and then the men were shouting to him to come and see Freya. It was as if she were in a trance, or even having a fit. He had been distraught, for they all truly loved her.

'Eventually he told me the Prince had just appeared. He had no idea how he knew where they were except that all the world seemed to have gathered in Jerusalem and with earthquakes and darkness nobody knew where anyone was.

"Yes, Aba recognised him, of course. Remember he had spoken to him of his desire to marry our lass, a couple or so of years ago and he told him he would consider again when she was older? It seems he was in Jerusalem with the one hope of finding her whereabouts but of course Aba had no idea of that at the time. The Prince says he had been praying, though he didn't know anything about prayer, or God even.

"Anyway, it was one of his servants who had found Freya in a daze, and wandering, not knowing her own name even, and so it seems the Prince had at once sent out a stretcher party, even before he had realised who she was, and not knowing what else to do had her brought to his encampment, there on the Mount of Olives, arranging to have her cared for, until she was sufficiently recovered.'

Maria and Prisca paused to exchange glances and a happy little embrace, realising how wonderfully fortune, or even some greater power, had been working on the behalf of their children.

'Oh, how gently he cared for her and wooed her, offering to marry her and take her to his estate here on his island, so aptly named Fair Winds.

'That is the story old Aba told me. This wasn't the time or place for me to throw accusations at him. I was almost out of my mind myself. Freya must have agreed, if she even understood, for somehow one morning your party had left, going one way, while our party managed to bring me safely back to my own home.'

Maria was intending to go on to say that out of that chaotic scene in the great city of Jerusalem, what great good had come for their Spice Maiden, when they each put their fingers to their lips as they heard the sweetest melody, - harmony rather. The Prince and his Princess were singing a lullaby to their precious, though as yet unnamed, son.

CHAPTER 11
UNFOLDING OF LOVE

There was a pathos in the melody, sweet and yet a little mournful too. Freya, having learned the tune from her beloved Prince, now began to intertwine some harmonies of her own, but then, instead of singing, there seemed to be a pause, -oh dear. Could it be weeping? The women knew this was the time for them to quietly slip beyond earshot.

If they would have stayed they might have heard Hermas continue, no longer singing, but speaking out the beauty of the words from the manuscript that was before them.

Her head was on his shoulder, and he gently caressed her as she wept awhile.

> 'Rise up, my love, my fair one, and come away,
>
> For lo, the winter is past, the rain is over and gone,
>
> The time of singing has come.'

Gradually he felt her sobbing subside and as he gently unrolled the scroll a little further their eyes scanned it together.

'Who was he, this Solomon, that he could write such a wonderful book?' Freya lifted her head to ask. 'It was the most wonderful gift any woman could have received from her husband.'

'Yes, especially from a husband who seemed to have abandoned his wife.' It was Hermas speaking now. 'I thought it had come from heaven to me. As I read it, somehow God opened my heart to understand how abandoned you might be feeling and how he was going to use it to bind our hearts together.'

'Abandoned! Yes, indeed, that *was* how I was feeling. When I came out of the terrible nightmare I had felt I was in, it was as if I had awoken into such a place of peace and love and care, it really seemed that all my dreams had come true. And then, my handsome Prince, you came and told me how you had first seen me in that market place in the land of Persia, such a long time ago. But of course I had only been interested in the pursuit of this wonderful fragrance at that time, and I was not yet ripe for love. And then again, when we were travelling up the King's Highway from Damascus, all of us on our way to Jerusalem, you told me that you had spotted me again and again you had that conviction that I was the one your heart had been seeking. But you found that my heart was filled with the desire to find the One who must be the fountain of this wonderful fragrance of which I had become so aware.

'Oh, my Beloved, over all these years you had been willing to wait and to watch over me from afar, but now that you had found me I was lost and it seemed all my hopes had been shattered. I had been so sure that this man Jesus, surely a God/Man, this Wonderful One, would have been willing to welcome us – but he didn't. Philip didn't really understand, but he knew he couldn't bring us to him, not then. And not long after that it seemed as if the whole world around us was disintegrating and we heard terrible rumours that this Jesus might be killed. It felt as if something inside me had died too, - I seemed to have lost my awareness of spices or perfumes, or even the desire to live and marvelled that you should have any desire for me, or thought I had any worth. But yes, I could understand that you were offering me protection and a home, and I was in need of this so much, so of course I could not refuse your offer.

'At last I would belong. Or so I thought. I knew I was only of value to Antonio, Aba as we called him, because of my giftings in the spice trade.

'I was happy to rest in your beautiful encampment and have your dear Prisca to care for me. I seemed to have lost all my feelings and didn't seem to care what happened to me – though I was vaguely aware that my dear Maria was not around, and I was sad about that. But, feeling lost and numb, I agreed for you to bring me to your beautiful kingdom here on this island of Fair Winds. But, but –' The tears were welling up again and again Prince Hermas gently comforted and waited until she felt able to continue.

'I'm sorry,' she gulped at last. 'but, but, - well, I've always believed I was valued for my gifts, and so when you helped me plan out all these gardens, and even the means to distil the perfumes, I became convinced that that was why you had wanted me, so that I could bring you yet greater riches, - and – and… '

Poor Prince Hermas! He would have been glad of a change of raiment, for his shirt was becoming soaked with Freya's tears, but he would not have dared to pull away from her at such a juncture. He drew her even closer.

'Come, my dear one. Tell me. Did you really think that I had paid your Aba a great price so that I might become yet richer through your gifts? No, no. Yes, he valued you, but they all truly loved and cared for you. All your Aba wanted was for you to be safe and cared for – and your dear Maria too, though she also was lost in all the confusion so she hadn't had the chance to agree.

'Actually, it was Antonio who felt he should pay *me* a bride price, and he did give me something which was of infinite worth to me – but come, you finish telling me what you wanted to say.'

Freya took a sip of wine and splashed some water on her face. She was a woman and knew that tears would not enhance her beauty.

'Yes, but you did not know the worst thing that I thought had happened. You were working so hard on the gardens, thinking that would please me, but I was afraid that I had lost my special sense of spices and perfume.

'This very special perfume that had seems to have followed me from my childhood. It was clinging to Philip, and got stronger as we travelled into Jerusalem, but then, instead of something beautiful there seemed to be a terrible stench ----. Oh, such a city is Jerusalem, so magnificent and grand in parts, and yet other parts squalid and unclean. And somehow I was only aware of this terrible stench, and then everything was getting dark, even though it was only afternoon, and then the earth was shaking and it became darker than the blackest night....'

The Prince waited, but Freya seemed to have left him. He shook her gently. 'Yes?' he asked. 'What happened then?'

'I don't know. I must have fainted. I don't know. I remember some men were carrying me on a bier and a woman – perhaps it was Prisca, I don't know, was leading them, and then you came and led us into a tent and I thought maybe I was in heaven with people fanning me and giving me fruit and drink and Prisca like a mother to me and after some days of delirium, just sleeping and feeling safe, but still this aching sadness and knowing something terrible happened so that when you all packed up the tents and set out on the journey here to your island kingdom I didn't care much because of the great sadness in my heart.'

A servant came with a platter of fruit and called them to the house.

'And after luncheon you must rest, My Beloved, for we have travelled far with our memories. And after you have rested it will be my turn to be the story teller, for I have something very special to tell to you.'

Freya, her arm in his, lifted her face to her Prince, as if to demand the story now but he pressed his finger to her lips. 'It is a story worth waiting for,' he assured her.

CHAPTER 12
THE PRINCE TELLS HIS STORY

And indeed, she had to wait, for a message had come from the port. Hermas was called away, the little Prince Pilipas was feeling the pain of his first tooth appearing and making noisy demands for attention, so neither Maria nor Prisca, let alone his mother, had little leisure for reminiscing. But eventually the Prince had returned to share the night watches and a measure of order was restored.

It was in the freshness of an early summer morning that Freya and her husband, their tiny son still sleeping in his cradle between them, were seated on the veranda overlooking their estate.

'You promised me a story, my husband, and I have been very patient,' she began. 'Is this a good time for you to begin?' She moved the cradle slightly so she could reach across to caress Hermas. 'I trust it is a happy story.'

'What else?' he assured her. The baby stirred then, and she reached into the cradle to lift him to her breast.

'There now, we are all happy, and ready to listen. Aren't we, little one?'

A pause, and then Hermas began.

'Do you remember when this little fellow began to kick and at last you were sure that you had a child within you?' he asked. Freya nodded, wondering what was coming.

'I had thought you would have shared my joy, but instead, you seemed to be filled with fear. You were so tearful that I was concerned over what effect it might have on the child you were carrying.'

Freya shifted her child to the other shoulder as Hermas continued.

'I'm sorry, I was so slow to understand your fears, but eventually it dawned on me that maybe it was because you had grown up with this feeling of rejection; that your parents had been willing to risk, not only their own lives but yours too in their journey in search of these new spices. I pondered on this long and hard for I felt for you in this rejection. And so I wondered if it might be this that was causing you to fear that you could never make a good parent.' He stretched out his arm to embrace mother and child.

'For are we not one now?' Words were not needed to affirm this truth.

'Go on then.' Freya had to remind him of the story he was telling. 'So is this to do with why you had to go away?'

'Why, yes. I suddenly realised that I had something in my possession that might enable me to trace your parentage, and somehow I so hoped that it might even lead me to find out more about them that could give you assurance that they had indeed loved you.' Her eyes were wide now, questioning.

'Remember the little locket of myrrh that Antonio had taken from your mother's neck? He had recognised that it was silver and possibly of worth. It must have been a temptation to him to sell it for a great price. But then he looked to the future and began to think of how he could put it to good use as a bride price, to ensure a good marriage for this child they had all come to love dearly.

'Of course, I had no need to demand such a thing, but I was very happy to have it put into my keeping, realising it was something of your past, Dearest. And so, beginning to understand your need of assurance I set out on my journey with this as a key, not so much for your future, for no one could be better loved than you, my Beloved, but to somehow to open the door into your past.'

Freya shifted the child to her other breast, then gently rested her hand over that of her husband, thus assuring him that he had her full attention.

Again Hermas was quiet for a while, recalling the outset of his journey.

'I really didn't have much idea of where or to whom I should go, but I knew I must make for the mainland and was soon in all the chaos and hubbub of our great city. I wandered through the streets, then sat in a quiet garden, great temples all around. My head was in my hands. How could I know where to begin such a search? If only there was someone who could give me some guidance. I almost felt a longing that there might be a god among all the multiplicity of gods of the Greek and Roman deities, but I could not bring myself to believe in such things.

'I knew one could go into one of the many temples and consult an oracle, but somehow there was such a clamour coming from them of shrieking voices and jangling instruments that I knew I would not be able to trust their words, or even their seductions.

'But then I heard some voices, a solemn chanting, and low. I tried to catch the words but it was not recognisable to me. I stood up to see if I could tell from whence it came - and just then an impressive gentleman emerged from an alley way and came to pass through the courtyard where I was sitting.

'His eyes were downcast and he was quietly mouthing words, yet silently, but as he passed me he paused, hesitating, as if wondering if he were meant to speak to me.

'I made to rise, but instead invited him by a gesture to sit beside me. He still did not speak, but quietly took his place beside me, then turned as if waiting for my question.

'Sir', I began. 'I am a stranger here and in need of guidance, but all around me is noise and confusion, until I heard this chanting which seemed to be a language of peace, though it was not a tongue I understood.'

'The stranger sighed and stroked his long beard. 'Peace?' he queried. 'Oh that it were. That was the Hebrew language you may have heard, for we gather in our synagogue.' And he pointed to a low and insignificant building I could just see through the jungle of temples. He told me how they gathered together that they might not forget   their own language, nor the words that had been given them by their God, for though strangers in a strange land, they were still God's people.

'He would have gone on to tell me his story, but I had left my beloved wife without explanation and was anxious to find out her story, not his. Furtively I took out the precious package I had concealed within my garments. Making sure we were not watched I showed him the inscriptions.

'Sadly he shook his head. My heart sank, and his head too seemed to sink upon his chest, but then he raised it again.

'We are a people who treasure the words of our God,' he began.' 'And because many of our people are living now in other nations the wisest scholars are said to be gathering even now in a town in Egypt. They have a deep longing to translate our writings into the common tongue.'

'Greek?' I queried. He nodded affirmation. 'But this is not Greek.'

'Indeed. But these scholars are all linguists, the finest in the world. I would advise, if you are serious in your search, that you bring this writing to the attention of these holy men, for if anyone can help you I am sure you will find the answer among these students.'

'Oh husband,' Freya complained, 'this is such a long story, and yes, in truth you were gone a long time. But your son is in need of some attention. Could you not come quickly to the end of the story?'

'Be patient, my Freya,' Hermas pleaded, as he helped her stand and took the child from her. 'It is a truly wonderful story and I don't want to leave out any of it. We will have food and then you and the child must sleep through the heat of the afternoon. Then, I promise you, I will be waiting to continue with my adventures, for this is part of your story too.'

The lamps were lit, a screen protecting them from the cicadas and crickets that were filling the air with their busy if discordant songs, but the Prince Hermas was longing for the quiet within to continue his story. Now, at last, the child was asleep in the care of his nurse and Freya had eyes and ears for him alone.

'It was not long before we were able to take ship across the sea to the great port of Alexandria. This teacher from the synagogue, Demetrius was his name, had decided to accompany me, for he had great interest to see whether they had indeed been able to commence this work of translation.'

'The crossing had been rough, and my legs somewhat unsteady when we landed, but we were refreshed as we made our way out of the hubbub of the market place and he led me to some buildings up on the hillside where scholars were wont to gather.'

'Because my guide was known to them we were welcomed and refreshed. I was anxious to tell them of my mission, but Demetrius was equally anxious to impress me with all their scholarship and various manuscripts.'

'Was it there you were able to purchase the wonderful story of the Shepherd that you sent to me?' Freya interrupted.

'Why, indeed, yes,' her husband replied, marvelling that he should have forgotten such a vital link in their own romance. 'I was given this manuscript to peruse, even as I was waiting to meet with these certain scholars who had the skill to unravel ancient languages, and so I was able to enjoy this story and my thought travelled back to my village maiden, so concerned for the child she was carrying and who must have been feeling abandoned by the one who had pledged to give her undying love.

'Wonderfully, Demetrius was willing to spare his own devoted servant to carry it to you and to teach you how to read.'

There was a pause once again in his account as they embraced, rejoicing that so many misunderstandings had already been dealt with, but Hermas knew they must get to the end before something or someone else would interrupt.

'Come, Beloved, let me get to the end of my story, this part of it anyway,' for Freya had taken a footstall and was sitting now at his feet, her eyes upon her prince. But even now, he was the one who hesitated as jumbled memories flashed before his eyes. The chaotic streets of Alexandria, the wise ones he was introduced to – some who appeared more greedy for wealth than they were for wisdom and who showed an unhealthy interest in his little silver locket, so that he had to make sure that he was not being followed as he left them.

'It was a long, weary search,' he told Freya, 'but at last I found an old scholar who evidently had travelled far and had heard many languages. I was comforted that he seemed more interested in the inscription than the value of the silver. After what seemed a long time he looked up at me and told me, 'Yes, I do recognise this language, though it is an ancient script. It is still spoken, I believe, in a mountain kingdom, somewhere north of Macedonia.'

'I asked him if he could guide me there, but he shook his head, and of course I understood. He was an old man. Demetrius joined us and we talked over the problem.' He paused and they both listened anxiously as a whimper came from their son, but the nurse soon settled him and Hermas was able to continue. 'I was resenting every day that was keeping me from you, my Freya, but I knew I could not give up now.

'At last he arranged for me to join a band of traders, and he sent his own grandson to accompany me. After many adventures, for the roads were full of danger, - we were far from the security of Pax Romana, we took ship until at last we reached this mountain kingdom.

'We wandered through the villages, until at last we found a Greek speaker who was able to interpret for me. I began to share my story, and sometimes with many misgivings, showing the locket. When it seemed my search was hopeless I remembered how the old Hebrew scholar had spoken of his god. From deep in my heart I cried out to this god of the Hebrew people.

'It was the next day that I was invited to a farmstead up on the hillside. They had heard my story, and asked to see the locket. It was obvious that there was a connection. They chatted among themselves and others had been gathered.

'Yes, Dearest, I had to be patient, even as you are now,' for Freya had quietly risen, had a quick peek behind a curtain to see her child was safely asleep, then settled herself again close to her story teller.

'After their chat, to and fro, an older man, using our interpreter, told us the story. Yes, Beloved. It was concerning your parents.

'It seems they had known your parents. Your mother had come from another kingdom, a strange northern land. And she had a wonderful gift of healing. She would travel far to gather herbs and spices for healing remedies. A traveller from her homeland, an old seaman, had heard talk of some wonderful spice islands and this new nut which was rumoured to have healing qualities. She longed to find out if this was indeed true, but every means of possessing some seemed to fail. Though she had given birth to a child she begged her husband that she might accompany a party of adventurers who were going in search of this precious fruit. She was still breast feeding the child and was not willing to leave her in the care of another.

'Yes, she knew she was taking a great risk, 'But we must be willing to take such a risk in order that many others may find healing,' she had insisted.

Freya was weeping by now. 'Oh, my mother, my dear brave mother.'

Hermas was quiet for a while, remembering how the elderly folk had begun to gather, and to tell their remembrances of the beautiful young couple who had left them, so long ago, hoping to bring further blessings to their people. One by one they had recounted their own precious memories.

There was a young man, still rejoicing in the strength of youth. 'I had a withered leg,' he told them. 'The mistress had seen how I was struggling as I tried to care for my few goats and she asked me to come to her each day that she might rub her healing balm into my feeble limbs and as she did she would sing her own sweet melody. I could not understand the words, but I felt new life coming into my leg. And see, now I can work with the best of them.'

One after another they came. There was an elderly lady, on the arm of her daughter, now a healthy young matron. She had feared she would lose her for she was such a sickly babe, but after she was prescribed this herbal drink she had flourished throughout her life. 'Yes,' she told me. 'She has carried three of her own, and as a family we are all in the best of health.'

'But oh, there are others so greatly in need of her healing touch and her songs too.' Oh, oh, as the people continued to gather, how they had sighed and wept that the lovely Jedidah had never returned, to continue her ministry among them.

Hermas stroked the hair of the beautiful young woman, whose head was now laid in his lap. Surely she had inherited the gifting of her mother? He could have told those strange mountain people that he would bring his wife to come and minister to them in her mother's place. But had she this same gift? And this awareness of fragrance? Was this still with her, or was it something she had as a child, but had grown out of?

And if she indeed had the same gift, was he willing that she, like her mother, should risk all in the pursuit of this ministry? Surely it was his duty to protect her and her little son?

He was grateful when his wife stirred and stretched herself, and he could leave all these demanding questionings. He would do his best to bury them in the realm of forgetfulness. Life was sweet here in his island kingdom. Surely they had all they needed.

Yet though he lay in his hammock beside her, sleep evaded him for he knew that there was more yet to be told. But would he ever be strong enough to tell it? Oh, for the sleep of forgetfulness.

CHAPTER 13
THE PRINCE CONTINUES HIS STORY

Yes, Hermas had thought that he had found out all he could, and had been longing to return to his own kingdom and his rich inheritance in his family, but no, it could not be yet. There was more, for he heard that they had found Freya's own parents and that they had set out to come to him with their own version of her story.

He remembered they had seemed a wizened little couple, doubtless shrunken through suffering and the long, long years of hopeless longing, and yet now, as if through the wrinkles, there was a brightness coming to their eyes and a glimpse of hopefulness as they looked from the Prince to the silver container. Hermas had been an avid listener and gradually this is the story he was able to piece together.

It had been perhaps half a century ago that, in the remote mountains of Transylvania a child had been born who had seemed different from others. Brought up among these hardy people who laboured to make a living through their crops and stock in the greener valleys on the lower slopes of the granite ranges, this child would wander free, forgetting about the goats in her care as she clamoured among the crags to find some sweet herb, or follow a streamlet to gather the cresses that grew near a water fall.

Many a scolding she had for her neglect of the task for which she was responsible, but as she grew and her parents and others in her village came to recognise her skills, they would look to her to bring her healing balm for their wounds, or some herbal concoction that would ease a mother through child birth.

The day had come when, having grown into a beautiful, if somewhat unusual woman, the parents had watched with concern as she had refused the interest of their own village lads. But when a trader, having landed at the nearest port, and captivated by the beauty of their mountains, had come across this wayward maiden high up on the ranges, they could see that the stirring of love was awakened. Together the pair found a strange affinity and the parents could see that this stranger, young, strong and of course handsome, had won their daughter's heart. For a few months they had settled in a cottage among her own people.

When in turn, their grandchild was born her parents had thought them safely anchored, but no. The son in law, having returned to the nearest port on some pretext, had been lured again by the call of the sea. Was the lonely existence of a sailor's wife to be her sentence, as for so many? But no. For it was when he had shared with his own 'Spice Maiden' stories of these exotic nuts reputed to have healing power, discovered on some remote islands, that their only daughter had determined that she must accompany her husband.

Surely, surely they would not risk, not only their own lives, for the seas were perilous indeed, but the life of their precious grandchild?

But it seemed they had eventually come to the place of willingness, for it was they who had had their parting gift so preciously crafted.

Hermas recalled the tears that sprang so readily to the eyes of this elderly couple as they had come to tell him their story, and had taken again into their own hands the precious silver ampule. It was they who had been able to confirm to Hermas the meaning of the words inscribed so beautifully round its stem.

It had been the breakthrough he had longed for when someone had come to tell him of a wise woman who had some knowledge of ancient scripts. It was she who had directed them still further north, following the coast line to these ancient people. Before they had set sail again she had sent for him to tell him of a possible meaning of the strange inscription. When she told Hermas this translation he had felt a deep response within his heart. And now, so wonderfully, it was confirmed to him by the very parents of his beautiful princess.

'SEEK WISDOM,

SHARE WISDOM'

Yes, that was it. Having recounted all this to his Freya, that night Hermas tossed and turned in his bed. Again he felt that somehow a greater being was speaking into his heart and that this was a word for this time and for his own heart.

Perhaps this was what he needed to do more than anything else.

He slipped from his bed, for sleep was eluding him, as he thought of the great pain of this now elderly couple who had had to be willing to part with their precious child, and now grandchild – to be willing to share them in their pursuit of a healing ministry.

'Seek Wisdom

Share Wisdom.'

Surely this was what they had done in releasing their beloved daughter, Freya's mother to this search which for them too had had such a tragic ending.

Hermas had already told Freya so much of his story, and her story too. But why had he not as yet told her that this couple, who were indeed her own grandparents, were still alive, still mourning for their beloved daughter, and indeed for her too, and that they had eventually travelled so that he might meet them. Why had he not told her this?

Why indeed? Did he realise what conflict again might arise if he did tell her? What a wonderful reunion there might be for them, not alas with their own beautiful daughter, but with her own child, the beloved grandchild they had once held in their arms, and had parted from so fearfully, now restored to them after so many years.

Yes, but if he did tell her, and she wanted to travel to meet up with them, was he willing to risk the lives of his wife and child as they made this yet another perilous journey, in order for them to be reunited? And as she heard of her Mother's undoubted gifting in the realm of healing, what burdens would this be placing on his Freya?

After a troubled night Hermas grabbed a robe and wandered out into the coolness of the breaking dawn. A solitary bird began to pipe its lonely call, but in the olive grove one might have seen the young prince kneeling beside a fallen tree.

CHAPTER 14
NEW BEGINNINGS

Dawn had broken and the household now astir when one sound broke into the meditations of Hermas. He stretched himself uneasily from his vigil, for the voices echoed anxiety, and he had been somehow in another place where he was being challenged to enter into new realms and purposes.

The voices seemed to be all around him. Then one voice, that of his beloved, pierced his consciousness, but it was not his name that he heard called, but that of their son, the little Pilipos who, having gained some control and strength in his chubby legs, was now capable of wandering far.

He made toward the house to see the Princess Freya, grabbing a robe, and her hair tumbling around her, as she too had been disturbed from her slumbers. She threw herself upon her husband.

'Oh, Husband,' she gasped. 'I woke to see your hammock empty, and I was not disturbed as I know you sometimes like to greet the dawn, but then I saw our child too was not in his little bed. I thought maybe he had followed his father, ...' She began to shake and the tears spurted from her eyes.

Maria was there now, and the Prince released her to her foster mother as she held out her arms to embrace her. 'Oh, my little Spice Maiden. I believe the child is his mother's son, for I have an idea of where we may find him.' Taking Freya by the hand she led her, the Prince following, wondering, up through the formal gardens that were near the house, to where there was a fragrant plot that Freya had once begun to plant out but then had left it abandoned for many months.

There, as Maria had surmised, she spotted the little lad picking some of the leaves, rubbing them in his hands and then holding them to his nose.

'Mama, Mama!' the little prince reached out his stained hands to his Mother that she too might enjoy the fragrant oil he had discovered.

Embracing the lost lamb, the parents both looked to Maria, questioning.

'Why yes, My Lord, My lady – ' she was always careful to give honour to the one who was as dear to her as if she had carried her in her own womb, when Freya was with her husband, or even in the presence of others.

'I have noted how your son is so like his mother at his age. She so loved to be in my kitchen, or where they were cooking by the road side, and would savour one spice or perfume or another. She was the same among the herbs in my garden. And somehow I felt a nudge that he might have found this special bed of fragrance that my Lady had planted, even though she has so long neglected it.'

With the little Prince seated high upon his father's shoulders, a thoughtful party made their way back to the house.

Even before any rebuke or chastisement could be metered out, a weeping nurse maid had fallen at their feet, begging forgiveness that she had not guarded her charge more carefully. Both Freya and Maria too had assured the contrite girl of forgiveness, and she was thankful that she was not banished, though given lower status in the household.

Neither parent would let their son out of their sight throughout that day. Indeed he was delighted to be able to lead the way from fragrance to delightful fragrance, but after they had all rested through the heat of the day it was Freya who now was leading the way to some of her hidden bowers.

When at last the tousled head was laid to rest, and this time safely guarded, Hermas took Freya by the hand and led her out onto the balcony, the hills around glowing in the fading light.

'Oh, my Spice Maiden, at last I have you to myself, for there is much about which we need to talk.'

Freya was again in tears. 'Oh, husband, Forgive me that I should have been so negligent of our child,' she began, but Hermas was quick to reassured her.

'I do not blame you, Dearest, for am I not equally responsible? But there is much I need to tell you, and I believe that some divine being has spoken into my heart to give me boldness.'

Freya led the way to a bench where they could sit comfortably, that she might give her undisturbed attention.

Hermas reached out to caress her hand before he began.

'You know that having you as my wife is the most precious gift in my life. It was not by chance that I first caught sight of you, there among the spice merchants, away in the eastern lands. You know how the thought of you was always in my heart, so that, in spite of my parents scheming and manipulations I could be satisfied with no other. And then, beyond all possibility, and in all the darkness and tumult in the old city of Jerusalem, I not only found you, but you were placed into my care.

'The situation was far from what I would have wished, but though you did agree to come to my kingdom here and to be my wife, I knew that, because of your strange illness I had to be very patient to win your love.'

His story was interrupted as Freya snuggled even closer to her husband, responding with kisses of glad assurance that her heart was truly won.

'But you remember that I left you for many months, my Beloved, and it was at a time when you so much needed my presence, and yet there was a need that I felt must be met.'

Freya was alert, wondering what was coming, for had she not heard this story before?

'Once you were sure that you were with child, do you remember you had this great fear that you would not make a good mother, because you felt your own mother had not loved her child, since she had taken you on this perilous journey putting all of your lives at risk?' Her caress assured her affirmation.

'My dear one,' the Prince continued. 'I have gone to great effort to be able to bring you assurance, and I know now that it was not just my human effort that enabled me to at last locate your grandparents, and I believe it was not just for your sake, but for theirs too that I was at last able to meet with them.' Yes, of course he had been compelled to share this too with his Spice Maiden. But he continued.

'My Freya, you must believe now that it was because your mother knew she had this special gift of healing that she faced such great dangers. And we have no reason to know whether she knew that she already carried you in her womb when your parents set out on this journey. Or if she did she would have been well aware of the risk she was taking in insisting you both share in the adventure. And we can but imagine your parent's great concern for you as they took to this dangerous sea passage.

'Oh, my Freya, surely you cannot doubt your mother's love for you any longer, or that you are not a good parent? That we are not good parents? Yes, I know our Pilipos slipped through our defences this morning, but I believe even this was allowed that we might realise that he has inherited the love of herbs and healing from his grandmother, - yes, and from you too, though you insist that you have lost it.'

Since no response came from his wife, who seemed to be snuggling deeper into his arm, he turned and lifted her face, only to see that yet again the tears were flowing. Calling to one of the servants to bring the little prince from where he was happily dabbling among the lavender, he lifted his wife and carried her to the house, laying her on a divan in the shade of the veranda.

The household slept through the sultry heat of the afternoon, until Freya was awakened by gentle caresses from her child, as well as the fragrant aroma that told them that supper time was near.

'Is the Prince returned?' she asked the servant who had come to remove the awnings and was beginning to spread the table.

'I believe he has gone to walk in the hills,' she replied. 'I'm sure he will be back before night falls.'

But night fell quickly, and some of the men had already gone out with lanterns to guide their master before Maria slipped in to assure the anxious Freya that all was well.

'No, he said he would not eat now. He has gone to bid good night to the child, and he would talk with you later.'

How relieved Freya was when at last her husband came to her, where she reclined on the veranda, to see that there was no sign of stress on his dear face, though she knew she had given him grief by her tears earlier.

The racket of the cicadas and chirping of crickets was all that disturbed their peace as they sat hand in hand, knowing their love for each other was sufficient to guard them from any discord.

At last the Prince broke the silence. 'I have been alone in the hills, my Freya, and yet I knew I was not alone. For so long I have refused to acknowledge the many gods of the Romans, yet I cannot help but be aware that there is a great power that is working for good in our lives.

'Somehow I could not doubt that it was because this power was guiding me that I was at last able to trace your family, and yes, even to understand something of your giftings.'

So, what revelation had been given to him, to them? Was there more to this story?

CHAPTER 15
STRANGE NEWS

It was confidence in the love of her mistress, and of her child too, that had given Maria boldness to approach the master. He was walking back now from the vineyards where he had been consulting with his supervisors.

'What is it Maria?' he asked as she struggled to rise from the bench where she had been waiting.

He directed her back and came to sit beside her, knowing if they walked she would have no breath left for talking.

His overseer discreetly continued up to the house and Hermon knew Maria would now be free to say what she wished.

'Master,' she began, 'You know that we all love your beautiful Princess. I love her as my own child, and yet I know that none of us have loved her as you love her. It is with confidence in the strength of your love that makes me dare to speak to you.'

'Well?' Hermas waited, wondering. Was there more this wise little woman expected of him?

'It was for love of your Freya that you have travelled far and through danger and difficulty, even to giving up being with her to see your son born ....

The Prince was about to speak up in his defence, but Maria held up a finger.

'Oh, forgive me, my Lord, but please let me have my say, for it has taken me much courage to come and speak to you like this.' By a gesture the Prince showed that he was listening.

'My Lady has told me all about her parents and that she knows now that she was deeply loved and that her own mother was one who had a great love, not only for her own family but for all those who came across her path.'

'Why yes, Maria,' the Prince interrupted. 'And it is evidently a gift which has been inherited, for it seems our little prince has the same gifting…'

But Maria was not willing for his interruption. 'But yes. This is my concern. This is why I wanted to speak to you. The family gift is undeniable, and yet it seems our Lady is not willing to pursue it again. She does not go with the child to the gardens, however much he tries to drag her there. It is I or Prisca, with the younger women of course, who must accompany him, while the Princess Freya, though she is deeply satisfied with the love of her husband

and child, and yes, with the love of those of us who serve her so gladly, yet she still seems to be in mourning....'

'But what is it then?' The prince could not be silent any longer, but Maria had not finished unburdening herself. She slipped from her seat and knelt before her Master in her earnestness that she might be heard, even though her limbs were not so supple these days.

'Our Spice Maiden, from a tiny child, had this same delight in various fragrances, even as her son, our little Prince, but there was something more.'

'Yes?' Hermas leaned forward as if he would draw the story from her throat.

'It was around the time when you first saw her.'

'In the land of Persia?' Maria nodded. 'It was around this time the Captain had told us to dress her as a boy, for the plain little bud was fast emerging into the fullness of blossom. So she was mingling happily, unrecognised, when she became aware of this wonderful fragrance – something so much more than anything she, or any of us, had known.

'It seems that she first became aware of it when she met the lad who had brought a sample of saffron to the market. You have heard the story of how she met this Wise One who told her the story of how they had seen his star and travelled far to worship a new born king. They had taken their most valuable fragrances of myrrh and frankincense as gifts, but it seemed that they had returned with a different perfume of which it seems they themselves were unaware, and yet our little one was wonderfully aware.

'Perhaps this awareness was only for the chosen, for when we came to Egypt, there was a little town where once again she perceived this same fragrance, and we learned that it was there that this same infant king had been carried there because the family had fled there as refugees from the wicked Herod.

Again Hermas tried to interrupt. Surely he had heard these stories, but Maria clasped her hands in supplication, thus begging that she might continue uninterrupted.

'It was many years later, as you, my Prince are well aware, when we were on the Spice Road. We were returning from Damascus when we met other travellers on their way to the city of Jerusalem, and were advised to make our way there because of the great skill of the Jews in the mixing of aromatic spices for their altar of incense to offer to their God.' Hermas half rose to go, but Maria resisted him.

'Well, if there is an end to this story, Maria,' he complained, 'at least come and seat yourself again, or you will lose the use of your poor knees.'

After struggling to obey and having regained her breath, Maria continued.

'I am nearing the end, my Lord. You see, we continued now our journey in the company of other Greeks who had travelled with the specific purpose of attending this special feast that was held in Jerusalem at that time of year. Well, you know about that, for you too were there. And there was a young man who was telling us all about it, and then he started to talk about this young prophet who was teaching about God, and doing wonderful miracles. And as he was talking I could see that something was happening to our Freya......'

Again Hermas went to interrupt, wondering how long the story would be, but Maria tried to assure him that she was getting to the crux of her story.

'It is really important, my Lord. I will try to be brief.'

Hermas chuckled. He knew that Maria and brief did not go together. He tried to breathe deeply and trust that this *was* going somewhere.

'It was when we reached a village in the outskirts of Jerusalem that she was aware of the fragrance again, and there we were welcomed by a woman who had been healed by this Healer. Jesus was his name. We learned he too had come for the feast and we met this man Philip who was actually one of his followers and was going to arrange for us to meet this Jesus. Freya felt that this was to be the culmination of all her life's journey.'

Hermas waited, but it was as if Maria had fallen into a trance. 'Well?' he demanded.

'Well,' she responded. 'All was not well. We didn't get to see this Jesus, as you know. Philip came to apologise. He said he did not understand. He had never known his master to turn away any seeking souls. Jesus had said something obscure about how a seed in the ground has to die to bear fruit. And then – well, you were there too, Master. There were all these rumours, and the terrible darkness. It all seemed to overwhelm our maid. It was as if it had affected her sanity. And I had not stayed with my lamb. We were all distraught and Aba sent me off to seek help for Freya but then ended up helping a woman in labour,' she added by way of explanation as Hermas looked accusingly at her. 'And of course, you know more than I of what followed.'

'Yes, yes.' Hermas seemed quite testy as he confirmed this. 'I, too, seemed to have been drawn to this special festival, but fortunately my servants had found a place far from the actual city to set up my camp. All I know if that my Prisca and her husband had come across Freya wandering, apparently out of her mind and they had brought her here to me, asking if we might care for her.

'I could hardly believe that it were possible that this maiden I had loved for so long should be here, seeking my shelter.

'But come, Maria. We all know this story. But what I want to know is, why? Oh why are you telling all this to me, and now?'.

Again Maria pleaded with the prince to be patient.

'Oh, my Lord. Don't you see? It had all seemed like the stories our mothers used to tell us when we were children, always with a happy ending.'

'Well, is this not our happy ending?' He stretched his hands out as if to embrace the whole of his island kingdom.

'Forgive me' Maria pleaded, 'but not quite yet, for I believe our Lady, to be fully healed, must have her gifts restored and once more be aware of this fragrance which seems to come from heaven.'

'But, -but, why are you telling me all this now?' Hermas asked.

'Well sir,' Maria hesitated.

'Yes, yes?'

'Well Sir,' Maria tried again. 'There is a rumour being spread abroad from some sailors who have put into port, that this Jesus had indeed died, as we had feared. He *was* crucified, but that wasn't the end. They say he has arisen again from death. People have seen him.'

They sat in silence, but since the prince made no response Maria eventually got up and trudged back to the house. Hermas sat on there for a long time. He had done, he felt, his utmost to delve into the past of his beautiful wife, to help to bring healing and joy. But it seems his efforts had not been enough. Was there yet a great price that he must pay?

CHAPTER 16
DAWN OF HOPE

'Has the Master been back for food?' Freya had awakened to realise his bed was empty. This was not unusual. Hermas always seemed to be an early riser, but when he had not returned for the midday repast she became a little concerned. However, they were united again over their evening meal and shared news of each other's day. She heard of how the crops were developing, of additions to the herd of goats that Justus cared for; even news from the town so near to the coast. She relaxed then, trusting there was no cause for concern.

But now, as Hermas questioned her concerning her day, it was the Prince who was concerned, for his wife told him of cloth they were weaving; of the gift of wine that had been sent from a neighbouring estate and was going on to tell him of some other project, but nothing concerning the gardens and more especially their little son, Pilipos. He felt he had to put aside the deep disturbance he had felt with Maria's news concerning this Teacher Jesus.

'But what of our son and heir? he asked, taking the little one on his knee. 'And what do you have to say for yourself?'

Pilipos seemed to be putting all his strength into growing strong legs, and was not so concerned with developing the ability to converse, for he could get by with taking someone by the hand and by gesticulating to have his demands met.

After some affectionate embraces, ensuring the child of his delight in him, the Prince clapped his hands and handed his son into the care of Prisca. The child went to her happily and Freya had had to rise to make sure that she too had her last embrace.

Hermas waited until the child was out of earshot before he reached out for Freya's hand.

'Beloved, what is happening?' he asked. 'You have regaled me with stories of your day, but no mention of time you have spent with our child.'

Freya withdrew her hand from her husband's grip. 'You know how he seems to be obsessed with the gardens, and Mycos, the garden boy, loves to teach him how to work beside him.' 'Yes, yes,' Hermas interrupted, 'but you should be there, taking an interest in all he is doing.'

Freya hid her head in her hands. When Hermas realised that yet again she was sobbing, he changed his tone and held out his arms so that she was snuggled up beside him. Once he had quieted her, she began to speak.

'Oh, my husband. Must this always come between us? I know that Maria and Aba, and now you too, are convinced that I have this gift – and now even this news that my own mother had such a gift, but – that does not mean I still have it. Maybe it is gone.

'All through my life I seem to have been able to detect this special perfume that is always connected to the story of the life of this one.'

'Jesus?' Hermas asked. She nodded. 'And then, it was gone. We had been so sure that this Philip was going to arrange for us to meet him, and that was to have been the beginning of a wonderful new life. But it didn't work out, and somehow the grief was so great that the only way I can find peace is to leave every part of that life behind me.'

There was a pause as he caressed her gently, a wealth of meaning in his action. 'And so God brought you to my tents that I might be used to lead you into a new life. And you too have been used to lead us together into a new life, and Beloved, it has indeed been a new life of joy and deep satisfaction – ' but even as she responded, her prince continued, 'though I think we both know that our cup is still not full, for until you are fulfilled and happy, then neither am I.'

Freya pulled away from her husband and began to pace the room. It was almost anger that tinged her words.

'How can I be truly happy? I know, I know. I have everything a woman could long for. A noble and loving husband, the most idyllic of homes, and loving servants, and most of all our beautiful child..'

'Yes?' Hermas, also on his feet, waited for her to continue. 'So why is it not possible for you to be happy?'

The tears began to well up. 'You know as well as I do,' she sniffled. 'They killed him. He is dead.'

'And so there is no more hope in the world?' Freya nodded, unable to speak.

'But there is a rumour going abroad that he is not dead. Yes, yes, I know. He was dead. There is no doubt about that; but suppose, just suppose that he conquered death and has come back to life?'

He could see that his wife wanted to rise up and deny such wonderful possibility, but she did not. She walked onto the veranda, and when eventually she turned to face him, he could see the light of a dawning hope on her face.

CHAPTER 17
A TIME OF SINGING

The next few days the Prince was busy assigning a new arrival of labourers to work in his vineyards, for it was almost time for harvest. Then it was time for the olive harvest, and cart loads of the luscious fruit were loaded into carts and taken to the port. Freya understood when he often excused himself from taking his meals with her.

Often it must have been that she was asleep before he came to bed and so, unwilling to disturb her, he had slept on the balcony, for the nights were warm, and when she awoke her husband was already up and out again working on the estate. So it was that it had not come as a great surprise to hear that Hermas had already set out on yet another long journey, leaving a note for her, with her own Maria.

'Beloved,' he had written. 'I have received word that a ship is in harbour that will take me on board so that I might make a necessary journey. Be at peace, my Freya, and care for our Treasure while I am away, and I believe the true God will bring me safely back to you, for I seek a medicine which will bring healing to broken hearts.'

Freya had waved away the servant who brought her food, for she was reading and rereading the parchment.

Why? Where? What? She had so many questions, but when Pilipos came, clambering onto her knee and demanding, 'Abba?' she knew she needed to give him her full attention.

The child had been happy, always escorted by a willing servant, but with her son now so obviously missing his father, she knew that this was no time to leave him to the care of others.

Delighted that he now had his mother in tow, Pilipos was in no doubt of where he wanted to go. Collecting a little trug and some tools to carry in one hand he firmly led his mother out to the newly laid flower beds lower down the slopes.

With few words and many gesticulations he demanded a rug to be spread out for his mother, but it was not long before she left her role as an onlooker, for her son had his little arms plunged into a bush of lavender and very soon she was beside him and revelling with him in the pungent aroma.

Some of the flower heads were already drying and so she deftly twisted a broad leaf to make a little cup and dropped in the dried lavender that they might carry it back to the house to be stored.

Forgetting her long held conviction that she had lost all awareness of perfumes, Freya had become totally absorbed in this new interest, until it was she who was discovering other fragrant plants, and gently preparing ground where they might have room to grow and thrive.

Maria and Prisca had come in search of their mistress and though delighted to see her gift awakened, were too wise to comment. Prisca quietly ran back to the house to see that a tray of refreshing juices and raisins were brought out for the labourers, while Markus, one of the wise gardeners, had also appeared on the scene to make suggestions of other additions they might make to this special garden of fragrance.

A lad, a few months older than the little prince, had happily joined their party and was showing Pilipos how to rub certain leaves in his hands so that he was soon to become a little green man, who smelled most deliciously of lemon.

Days passed, and there was no news from Freya's husband, but instead of the days being long, lonely and fear filled, Freya was awakened from refreshing sleep by the patter of little feet, little hands pulling her wrap from her and urgent cries of 'Mamma, Mamma, come, come.'

Pilipos was, of course, swiftly followed by Prisca, or one of the servant girls who would whisk him away, giving Freya some leisure to prepare herself to face the day. She and her little son had a glass of fresh goat's milk and freshly baked rolls, but once that was over off he marched to don his gardening apron, his little boots and then pick up his trug, especially made the right size for such a little fellow.

'We make garden' he would proudly announce to all they met on the way, and day by day it seemed to be that more and more were following. Demetrius had detailed one of the men from the estate to be on hand for any strenuous digging, while another, skilled in the care of herbs and flowering shrubs would be ready to give advice, for they were ever extending borders for the pleasure of the young but very demanding prince.

Dear Maria, who would be brought a seat so that she might be there as an encourager, would smile to herself as she remembered an equally sturdy little one who would empty the contents of her jars and lead her from stall to stall in the market as she came across wonderful smells. And yes, her own little patch of earth had soon been filled with clumps of sage and mint.

But however great Freya's joy in her child, she still had a great ache in her heart for the presence of her Beloved. Sometimes Maria would peep in to find her dear Spice Maiden weeping. She would fetch a cup of spring water and, bringing it, gather her in her arms and gently seek to reassure her. Then she would brush her long golden hair and as she brushed she would hum a tune that she knew the prince and his bride would often sing together.

'Open to me, my love, my dove,

For this is the time of song

The winter is past, rains over and gone.

Come, this is the time for song.'

It wasn't long before Freya was singing, and oft-times the little Pilipos would run in, snuggle onto his mother's lap and add his own tuneless harmony. By now he did not want to go to his garden without his own Mamma.

One morning Freya was humming quietly, even before she was out of her bed, but then, a light garment around her, she slipped onto the veranda and began to sing, and as she sang she swayed, lifting up her arms, and by the time Maria, and Pilipas too had joined her, she was dancing in an ecstasy of joy.

Poor Maria. Freya took her in her arms and attempted to twirl her around, but Maria had to cry out for mercy, collapsing onto a divan.

'Oh, oh!' she cried. 'My dancing days are over. But what is it, my dear?' she asked, as the girl sank down beside her.

She had gesticulated to one of the servants to bring refreshments, and the little Pilipos had trotted away with her. So now she drew her arm around Freya but was dismayed to find she was now shaking with sobs.

'Oh, my dear, my dear' she began. Would there be no end to her tears? She never even remembered her crying as a child. She had seemed always so resilient, but she had been coming to understand that somehow now she was coping with the grief she had not dealt with as a little one. But surely enough was enough. Freya however was struggling to speak. 'It is tears of joy, Maria,' she assured her when the sobs eventually subsided.

'Well?' A tray of refreshments had arrived and they had both made a good breakfast, but Maria was still waiting for some explanation.

'Oh Maria,' she began, 'oh, oh, I am so happy I don't know how to tell you.'

Again Maria had to wait. She could hear the child approaching, about to demand the attendance of his mother, but she gesticulated to a servant to keep him at bay.

'Oh Maria, I had such a wonderful dream. I dreamed I was walking in a field of lilies, and the fragrance was, oh so wonderful.'

'That's …..' Maria began, but Freya was begging her not to interrupt. 'But – but, what was so wonderful was, that when I awoke the perfume was still in my nostrils.'

Maria could not quite grasp the significance of what she was telling her but the demanding Pilipos could be kept waiting no longer. Freya, now suitably dressed, was once again happily at work on the garden project, while dear old Maria was glad to sit on a bench in the shade.

Her thoughts wandered to the Prince. How they longed for some news.

CHAPTER 18
THE PRINCE'S SEARCH CONTINUES

Prince Hermas stood at the bow of the sturdy vessel that was carrying him away from the mainland, where he had spent some days visiting his parents. But he was well aware that this ship was carrying him still further away from the island where, with his Freya, he had at last found a home for his heart.

He was a seasoned traveller, but though he had mingled with other merchants, especially on the Spice Road, acquiring many treasures to enrich his own kingdom, it was not until he had caught sight of his own Spice Maiden that he felt he had come truly alive, even though at that time they had tried to disguise her as a youth. But her beauty could not be hid, and from then on she was the desire of his heart, and his travels had only one purpose.

It had seemed such an amazing miracle when he had caught sight of his Spice Maiden, some years later, when he, and she too, with the Spice traders, had been strangely led to come to the Holy City. But on that occasion Jerusalem seemed a place of fear and confusion and his own heart filled with foreboding because of the seeming impossibility of his finding her again. Then, wonder of wonders, there they were, actually bringing her to his encampment, in need of his protection and care.

How had it all come about? At first she had seemed to be in a delirium, and even when she came out of it she had been so weak and ill that she seemed unable to care when he had offered her marriage, in order to care for and protect her. Old Antonio, the Spice Merchant, had been grateful to have her off his hands. But once they were settled back on his island it had taken much patience for Hermas to eventually win her love, for she had agreed to be his wife, feeling she had no option but to accept his protection. With all the turmoil in Jerusalem and separated from her dear Maria as well as the others, she had felt helpless and abandoned.

But now, how great had become their joy in each other, and in the little Pilipos too, the fruit of their love. So why, oh why was he here now, putting his own life at risk and leaving his Beloved sad and lonely while he was setting out on this, yet another journey, for where and what and why?

The sails were filled with a soft breeze, the oarsmen able to rest, while the captain, able to leave the navigation to one of his seamen, had turned to converse with his imposing guest.

'Yes,' he agreed, 'The weather is our friend now, but we never dare trust it, for so quickly a storm may arise and disaster come upon us. Why, we recently called in to the island of Melita and they told us of a ship which had been blown onto the rocks there. They were still collecting the planks and spars washed ashore from the wreckage. Of course it was winter time, and the captain had been warned that it was unwise to travel, but some people learn the hard way.'

'There must have been great loss of life?' Hermas asked, never doubting a positive answer, but his attention was held when the captain told him, 'No indeed. They had all thought it an amazing miracle. For days they had had to run before the storm, with no idea where they might end up, fearing the worst. Then the ship had run onto the rocks, and yet not one life was lost.'

Hermas, awe-struck, waited for some explanation. 'Have you heard about these Christians?' the captain continued. Hermas shook his head.

'Well, I don't know much about it, but it seems there was a man whom many of the Jews thought was their Messiah. The Christ, some called him. They are named after him. Sounds as if he was a wonder worker and they expected him to lead them against the Romans, but he ended up, as all do who are a threat to Rome, - yes, you know their cruelty – on a cross.'

Hermas interrupted him. 'Why, yes. There was a lot of talk about one Jesus, a carpenter's son, but we heard he was killed. We were in Jerusalem at the time. It affected my wife so grievously; she is not yet fully recovered. But what can he have to do with what happened on Melita? This man was crucified, yes and buried by his followers, we heard, and nobody recovers from death by crucifixion. And yet, I have recently heard a rumour that this Jesus, or Christ as you say, has indeed come back to life.'

The captain interrupted his story to shout instructions to his crew, for a bank of cloud had now spread out to cover the whole sky, while a surging wind was tearing through the rigging. He managed to shout to his passenger to take cover in his cabin.

A burly sailor had Hermas by the arm, but by the time he was safely sheltered he was soaked through and gasping for breath. Lying on his hammock he felt the rocking of the vessel, and the occasional crash as the mighty waves sought to toss the ship, only to throw it down again, like a child's toy. Hermas was not so much troubled for their safety as the thought of his beloved Freya, and little Pilipos. Would he ever see them again?

There was a mighty crash! The door of his cabin let in a torrent of water, but he felt himself lifted in strong arms, then it was as if he were being handed down through a manhole into the depths of the ship, where bales of cargo were sliding about.

Hermas looked to see who it was who had so easily manhandled him to come below, but though there was no natural light there seemed to be a glow around the stranger that dazzled him.

'Who are you?' he managed to ask him, but the strong one did not answer his question. Instead he began to relate the story of another storm. 'There is a story well known by the Jews of one Jonah who was found in the bowels of a ship in a terrible storm. He knew the cause of the storm. It was because he was running away from his God, so he told the sailors to throw him over the side of the boat and then the storm would cease.'

'What kind of God is that?' Hermas asked.

'A wonderful God, full of compassion,' he answered. 'Listen to the rest of the story. For as soon as he hit the water, the sea was quiet…' 'But at the cost of Jonas being drowned,' interrupted Hermas. 'Was that compassion?'

'Yes, for no, Jonah did not drown. His God has sent a great fish to swallow him and carry him in his stomach back to dry land, so he could go to where he had told him to go in the first place.'

'How could he survive being in the stomach of a fish?' Again Hermas interrupted. The ship was still tossing so violently that he needed to concentrate on his own stomach.

Next thing he knew, some of the crew were looking down on where he was lying on the floor of his cabin. Someone was dabbing a cloth on a wound on his forehead, and then it was the captain who had been called and now stood beside him.

'No, Prince Hermas, don't try to sit up as yet. You've sustained a hefty blow on your head. Stay quiet for a bit. The storm seems to have passed over for now, - Ahaz will stay with you till you have come to yourself.'

Hermas lay there, bemused. Had he been carried below or not? But someone had been telling him a story about so`meone called Jonah, or, or, he thought he had. The memory was fading, and now he wasn't sure if he was not back home in his island kingdom. He was filled with an incredible longing for his own little family.

Oh, my Freya, my little Pilipos. He longed to call out to them and to hear them respond.

The heaving of the ship had turned to a gentle rocking, but his queasy stomach assured him that he was still at sea.

'Prince Hermas, Captain asked me to tell you we are coming into the port of Joppa.'

'We had expected to make port further to the north, but we are thankful to have made safe harbour here,' the captain explained. 'We'll be here a few days so I can have some repairs done, and we'll hopefully do some successful trading while we are here. The storm blew us off course, but it is to your advantage, for this is probably the nearest you will get to Jerusalem.'

A few days of rest, thought the prince. I wonder if I can find someone that will carry a letter for me to my beloved?

The captain assured him that he would find a reliable messenger. He also suggested a tavern where he would find refreshing.

'You'll find good vitals there, and hear some good stories too. If old Simeon is there, ask him to tell you the story of the prophet Jonah.'

Jonah, Hermas pondered. Jonah? Had he heard that name before? Where and how? Having been safely escorted to the tavern and settled in his room, he called for writing materials.

'My beloved Freya,' he began. 'I have at last opportunity to write to you. How my heart longs for you, and our handsome Pilipos, but it is for your sake that I must continue with my journey, praying that very soon I may find something which will bring healing to my Spice maiden and restoration of your gifts. I had expected to arrive in the larger port of Caesarea, and make from there overland to Jerusalem, for I'm told that the most skilled perfumers in all the world dwell there, though whether they will share their secrets who can say.

'But first I want to ask you something, though I'm afraid it may be a long time before you will be able to answer me. Tell me, Beloved, when I sent the teacher to you that I met in Alexandria with the love story written by King Solomon, did he also ever tell you a story of a man called Jonah?

'Here in the port of Joppa, there is a story which has been passed on for generations, and it is said to be true, though I find it very hard to be believed.

It is of this man, Jonah, who was swallowed by a great fish and brought back safely to land, here in Joppa. He had been running away from his god when he took ship, but now, vomited up from the stomach of this fish, he knew he could no longer continue to run, and went to carry out the task he had been given to do.

'But now, what mystifies me in all this is that, I don't know if it was a dream or a vision, but when I fell in the storm a shining being came and spoke to me about Jonah, and how he was three days and three nights in the stomach of this fish. But if I had not heard of him before that, and now I find that it is a true story, then who was the shining one who came to me?'

Hermas continued to write over the next few days, until the tavern keeper came to tell him that a ship was shortly leaving for Greece and that a passenger had agreed to carry his letter. Also that a group of merchants were travelling over land to Jerusalem, and did he want to join them on this last lap of his journey?

Hermas gently felt the swelling on his head. Yes, it was fast healing and he could not return home until he had completed his mission. His heart longed for his family, but it was out of concern for his Freya that he had set out. Certainly he must accept this offer.

CHAPTER 19
NEWS FROM ABROAD

Back on their island Freya stood on her veranda and listened to the spritely tune that once again was tumbling from the pipe of their little goat-herd. Maria came and stood beside her. 'Now, don't get yourself excited,' she warned. 'You know it is far too soon to expect the good Prince home again.'

'Yes, I know that,' she laughed, 'but there is no harm in hoping. And it seems to be announcing *some* news, for all that. Maybe we should send a lad across to find out.'

Dear old Maria had been amazed at how contented her mistress had seemed with her husband away, while even she herself, the Princess Freya, had been surprised at how happily the days had been passing, though of course she longed for him.

'Mamma?' A little hand had slipped into hers and she looked into her son's expectant face. There he was in his gardening overalls, a trug and trowel all ready. 'Garden, Mamma?' he asked.

Certainly her little prince was the cause of the days slipping by so happily, for there was no doubt that her son had inherited his mother's awareness of herbs and spices and loved to be out in the gardens. Especially he and his playmate seemed to love the lavender, and they had had to direct some of the labourers on their estate to help with the weeding and then gathering so that when summer showers kept them indoors they found shelter in the sheds the Prince had prepared where the wonderful aromatic oil was being distilled.

Breakfast first, Maria commanded. They were seated together on the veranda with their platter of fruit, bread and cheese when a lad ran across with a little package and handed it to Maria, who, passing it to her mistress, then led him into the house to be duly rewarded.

'It seems a ship has just come across from the mainland with this letter. Is it from the Prince?'

How thankful Freya was that she had persevered in learning to read, and could enjoy her husband's loving messages all to herself, though she had to pause every now and again to assure her little son that yes, Papa had sent kisses for him. But soon others of the household heard of the excitement, and Freya found she was reading to an audience his account of the storm and safe arrival at Joppa.

There were gasps of wonderment when she came to the story of Jonah. Had any of them heard of this man? How could their master have heard of him before he had even come to Joppa?

'When the prince sent the manuscript of the Shepherd's Song, had he sent this story too?' Prisca asked. Freya shook her head. 'If only the teacher, Abba Beni were here, then we could ask him.'

The goat herd had arrived by now to share the news, and he threw in a suggestion. There are some people who have recently come to live in the village. They have a special room where they go to pray to their god, and they have special holy books, in their own language. We could ask them if they have heard of this Jonah.

One of his brothers was sent off to the coast. It was a few days before he returned. Maybe he had other interests in that little fishing village, but when he came back he explained that he had at last found this little group of people of Jewish ancestry who had become strong enough to be able to establish a synagogue and gather on their Sabbath to read from their holy books and pray.

No, they did not have the manuscript which had recorded the story of Jonah, but there was one of their company who knew the story and with some recompense would be willing to come and repeat it to them.

Freya discussed this with Maria and Prisca, always her close companions.

'Probably we know as much of the story now as he does, for the Master has already written his own account for us.' They discussed the matter to and fro, but in the end Freya agreed that they should pay for this man to come. 'We don't want to have any regrets.'

So it was, that a few days later, Freya and all of her household, as well as any casual labourers and contacts from the villages around, were seated around the veranda of the great house, listening to this foreign looking gentleman with the strange locks of hair, imposing hat and impressive garments.

'Jonah was a respected prophet of the Jewish people,' he began. They soon surmised that he also must be one of this nation. He continued.

'The great Jehovah, God of the Jewish people told him to go to Nineveh, the capital of the savage Assyrians, to proclaim God's mercy, if only they would repent. Otherwise God would destroy their great city. But it seems Jonah thought he knew better than God, so he reckoned that if he did not pass on God's offer of mercy, then God would have to destroy them.

'So, instead of going to Nineveh he got on a ship that would take him far away in the opposite direction. However, God intended him to take his message to the people of Nineveh. He sent a fierce storm, so Jonah went to hide right in the belly of the ship.'……… Ben Isaac, the story teller paused, for he heard a murmuring from his audience.

Freya was the culprit. 'That was what happened to Hermas,' she had whispered to Maria and Prisca. 'Only he wasn't really in the hold…' Prisca nudged her, and she apologised, allowing their story teller to proceed.'

'Jonah knew that it must have been his God who had sent the storm, so he tried to forget about it, as if somehow God would recognise that he was determined not to go and stop bothering. But of course we know he could not win a battle against his God.

'All the others on the ship were crying out to their gods and offering sacrifices to them, but when the captain realised that their passenger was not among them, he sent men in search of him, and there they found him, - would you believe? Fast asleep.

'Why aren't you praying to your god?' they asked.

'It is no use,' he explained. 'My God has sent the storm because of my disobedience.'

'Well, what can we do? We are all going to be drowned.'

'There is only one thing to do and that is to throw me overboard.' Give him his due, the captain was most unwilling, but eventually they did throw Jonah overboard, and to their amazement, a huge fish rose up out of the deep and swallowed the prophet whole, and of course they thought that was the end of him, but even more amazing, even as the fish disappeared within the waves, with Jonah and all, immediately the sea was calm, the sun came out and their sails were filled with a following wind.'

The story-teller continued with his story, and Freya listened carefully, realising that it was indeed the same story that her husband had been told by the captain, and then when he reached Joppa, but this still did not explain how he had first heard the story in his dream. But had it been a dream, or some strange, mystical experience? No, no, there must be some other explanation.

Their story-teller was being refreshed with food and drink before completing the story when a young lad ran up from their village on the coast with a message for the teacher.

He came to speak to Freya. 'My presence is required,' he apologised. 'It seems some visitors have arrived and have important news to impart to us and they need all of our company to be present before they will share it with us.'

Freya, of course, graciously allowed him to go, calling her steward to see that he was duly remunerated, and with his assurance that he would return to visit them as soon as his duties allowed.

It was some days before they heard any more from the Jewish community, but Freya was busy writing of all that had been happening, and especially of the recounting of the story of Jonah, in a letter to her husband, though who knew when there would be opportunity to send it, and indeed, who knew what amazing things would have happened on their quiet little island before she would sit down to write again?

CHAPTER 20
THE SIGN

Hermas knew that his destination was Jerusalem. Was it not there that he had again met up with the beautiful Freya, and yes, where she had agreed to become his wife, though he had to admit that it had been with little assurance. But something else had happened there, and it was for this reason he knew he had to make this journey.

 So it was that once again he had felt he had to leave his family, secure on their island kingdom, and make this dangerous journey, for something had happened while they were there in Jerusalem that had changed this care free maiden so full of hope and expectation into a woman who seemed to have fallen into a pit of despair.

But Hermas's heart had never changed toward the child, as she had been when he first met her, full of life, always seeking, always searching. Yes, when he met her again in the flower of womanhood, and he had taken her to his island kingdom, her heart had eventually been awakened to his love. And yes, she adored, as he did, their darling son Pilipos, their pride and joy. Miraculously, it seemed, Hermas had been able to make contact with her grandparents and through hearing their story now Freya could no longer doubt but that she had been truly loved by her parents, even though she could have so easily died with them in that terrible shipwreck.

'Died in a storm.' The similarity in the stories jerked Hermas back to his present situation, for he was still in Joppa, having taken lodging while seeking other travellers with whom he could travel on to the great city of Jerusalem.

An old fisherman sat beside him on the harbour wall as they watched the local fishing fleet set sale. He had once again heard recounted the famous story of how the prophet Jonah had set out, and so ignominiously was returned to Joppa, caste up on the beach from the stomach of a great but queasy fish.

Just then a lad ran up with news of a party of travellers who were setting out who would be glad to have him accompany them on this, the next stage of his journey. He sought them out in order to negotiating their terms, and then they were on their way on this long and often dangerous journey. Once they reached the King's Highway they felt more secure, for from time to time troops of Roman soldiers patrolled in order to secure the Pax Romana, and the prince felt more at ease to engage in conversation.

Some of the travellers were on their way to attend the feast of Passover in Jerusalem. Hermas knew of this, of course, for it was this time of year when there had been such strange occurrences, and especially for him the time when the paths of both he and his Freya had crossed.

Once again he was deeply interested to hear these travellers tell of the wonderful spices and perfumes that were used in the preparation of the incense which was such an important part of the offerings to their God. But he still had the story of the prophet who had been thrown overboard niggling in his mind, for how could this have been part of his dream unless somehow he had heard it before?

There was a family among the party of travellers. The grandfather was of concern to them, for he had insisted that he was able to make the journey, but he certainly did not have strength to walk and to talk. But now they had rested up at an oasis, and were glad to keep their Sabbath quietly.

Hermas sat respectfully nearby as they recited passages of the Torah together and then joined to sing some of the psalms. They invited him to share some of their meagre food, for they would not cook on the Sabbath, though others in the company had lit little fires. But then, after he was rested, the old man called the prince over to sit beside him.

'I heard you were interested in the story of the prophet Jonah?' he queried. In affirmation, Hermas repeated to him his strange experience while in the storm when he had received the blow to his head.

'And you say you had not heard the story before this?' He paused and gently stroked his beard as Hermas nodded affirmation.

'But you have been in Jerusalem before. Tell me when was this? Was it not the year that the young Prophet from Nazareth was crucified?' Hermas had spoken of this before. 'Oh, yes, indeed,' he responded.

'But there was so much talk of the prophet Jonah in Jerusalem, at that time, for there were many who believed that this Jesus was the Messiah. And it was well affirmed that when the chief priests had asked him to show a sign to confirm his claims, that he had said, 'there is only one sign that you can have and that is the sign of the prophet Jonas.''

'So what sign is that?' Hermas asked, even as he was processing the possibility that he might have heard of this, and that in his subconscious state it could have emerged to the surface. He listened intently now as the old man continued.

'Why, none of us understood at the time, though I expect his disciples had gone to ask the Master for an explanation. But of course, after it happened, then those of us who truly loved God and his word, understood.'

'After what happened?' Hermas questioned.

'Why, surely you have heard?'

'Heard what?'

'I do apologise for breaking into your conversation, but my father needs to rest,' and Hermas was left with nothing but questions hanging in the air. At least one problem was solved. The story of Jonas would have been on many people's lips on that occasion when he had previously been in Jerusalem. He must go and write this at least in the letter he was writing to his Freya, but there was obviously more to the story. What was it that this godly old man and his family had come to understand? How soon would he have opportunity to talk with him again?

He found consolation in writing to his Freya. Freya – how aptly named. Freya – fragrance. Even as he rested quietly it was as if the fragrance that he always associated with her was carried on a gentle breeze, breaking through the torpid heat of that Sabbath evening.

He was up early, knowing the Sabbath was over for these strange Jewish people, and the party would want to be off in the freshness of the dawn, in order to cover as many miles as possible before the sun reached its zenith. Hermas was looking forward to that time when they would seek shelter and a time to take some refreshment, for he hoped he might be able to sit beside the old gentleman and hopefully have some explanation of what it was they had come to understand, for oh, he so needed to know. But when they did stop to rest he searched them out in vain. It seemed they had left the party.

Hermas sat apart. He had woken with buoyancy in his spirit, but now his limbs ached and his heart was as a stone.

CHAPTER 21
NEW SONGS

But Freya woke with a song in her heart. She had every reason to be sad, for her husband was far away, and who knew what danger he might be facing? But her little son was at last soundly asleep after a restless night from some midge bites that he had acquired while in the garden.

She slipped onto a secluded balcony, gently brushing her hair as the words came to her from the old story her prince had sent to her from so long ago.

'My love, my dove, my spotless one

Arise and seek my face

Breathe deeply of my fragrance rare

Come, rest in my embrace

Here's spikenard and frankincense

All all for our delight

But fragrance rarer far than these

As faith leads on to sight'

Afraid to disturb her, her dear Maria had peeped around the screen to see if her Spice Maiden should wish for something. She soon understood her gesticulations that she required her writing pad.

With her stylus on the wax, Freya pressed out these verses, changing a word here or there, and then continued quietly singing:

'Oh do not turn your face away,

In me is beauty found

In me is fragrance and delight

For here is hallowed ground.'

Even as she was writing the last verse she had been conscious of music coming from over the hills. Yes, of course, it was their goat herd.

No, - not a message. She was conversant with them all by now, but this was something new; a sweet melody, though with something of a plaintive note.

'Listen, Maria,' she commanded, as dear, caring Maria, had crept in to place her breakfast tray beside her, guessing her mistress did not want to be disturbed. But, as often happened, with her mother heart, the old lady was there just when she was needed.

'Oh, I had wanted you to listen to the tune Justus was piping, but now he has stopped. Oh Maria, it was so sweet, and yet a little sad. I've never heard him play it before. – Oh, there!'

He had begun to play again, but again he stopped. Was he running after one of his wayward flock?

'I did not notice it, Freya, - oh, forgive me,- Madam.' But the lady's arms were outstretched to her. 'I am always your Freya' her mistress assured her. Maria continued.

'There has been something going on down by the coast, and Justus has been there. These strangers have come from the mainland, - not sure who they are, but people have been gathering to listen to them and Justus for one seems a changed boy.'

'It must be a change for the better if he has learned such a beautiful tune.' Freya affirmed. 'Can you send a message to ask him to come over once the goats are safely penned?'

The day seemed to be full of music, for the winds were blowing softly now, stirring a fragrance from the olive grove, as well as from her herb garden. This was where her son delighted to play, helping his especially appointed gardener, as he thought, while the man steered them carefully away from disturbing the seedlings they had helped him to plant.

That evening Freya was busy bathing the little boy, talking all the while about his father, and delighting to tell him how he had found her there in the market in a land so far away. Yet, no, she never told him anything of her strange beginnings, nor of her grandparents who must be longing to meet him. There were things still locked within her heart. Would she ever come to that place when she could happily share them?

CHAPTER 22

NEW LIFE

Freya woke the next morning with a great emptiness, longing for her husband. She tried to recall her special song, but somehow, though she had written the words, the melody would not come. Her little one had run to Prisca for comfort, having been spurned by his mother. Prisca and Maria united to give him comfort, but their eyebrows were raised. This was not like their Freya.

As Maria was brushing her hair, the subject of the goat herd soon came up. There had been no sign of Justin the previous day, nor one note of his melody, and it was not long before the tears were flowing as Freya confessed to her faithful friend her great longing for her husband.

'There, there, my lamb,' Maria sought to comfort her. 'I will send one of the lads running to see where that Justus is. If he can bring us a flask full of the wonderful joy he seems to have found, then I am sure your tears will soon be wiped away,' she purred, but the tears were not assuaged.

Maria could not remember her Spice Maiden indulging in tears, even from her days as a toddler, but somehow the unlocking of the memories of her parents had released the need to grieve. Yes, she understood, but how she longed for this fountain to run dry.

'What is any joy if my Prince is not here to share it?' she complained, but there was One as yet unknown to her who not only heard but was able to work a miracle.

'Hark!' Yes, it was Justus's merry piping, to say a ship was in.

'Now, now,' cautioned the faithful Maria, 'Don't go raising your hopes. He could still be many days or hours of travel away, even if his heart has responded to the cry of yours,' but one of Justin's brothers had come to the kitchen with a message from the goat herd to say he was off to meet with the strangers again tonight, but he would come as soon as he could to share their story.

Yielding to the pleading of her faithful Maria, Freya had spent a happy day with her busy little gardener, and now, fed and bathed, she had him on her knee as they sat together on the veranda, watching the fire flies even as the sunset's glow from the clouds was fading away. She was quietly singing as she rocked her little one, knowing one of her faithful servants would soon come and quietly take the sleeping child and lay him in his crib, but suddenly the child was wriggling in her arms.

'Abba,' he whispered, wondering, then acclaimed loudly, 'Abba, my Abba!' as strong legs leaped onto the veranda as first his child, and then mother and child were both secure in his arms. Eventually a sleepy, happy little boy was once more struggling to keep his eyes open and his Abba himself carried him to his crib. Now Freya and her prince were in a world of their own.

'Well, my husband, was your journey worthwhile? Did you find what you were seeking?' eventually she asked

Hermas seemed to be deep in thought, but then he pulled himself back into the present for she was waiting now for him to answer.

'Certainly, yes, it was worthwhile, but I went in search of healing for my Beloved, and whether I have indeed found that remains to be seen.'

Freya leaned into his arm, gazing expectantly, but again he paused, as if he did not know where to begin.

'You wrote to tell us of your dream, -or was it hallucination, after you had a blow to the head, but then you found everyone knew of the story..'

Hermas seemed to be on track now. 'Ah yes, about the prophet Jonah. But it was when I was travelling with some pilgrims going up to Jerusalem for the Feast, - remember?'

Freya did indeed remember, as he did too, though they had not travelled there together. How amazing, the way he had been there to rescue his Spice Maiden. But she reminded him now that he was telling a story.

'There were some devout Jews among this group of travellers, and one, an old patriarch, was going on to tell me something significant about the story of Jonah, but then, was he taken ill? I don't know, but the next day they had left our party.

'But when at last I got to Jerusalem, a godly family gave me accommodation, and they told me the end of the story. Oh Freya, listen to this!'

Oh, Freya was listening. Her eyes wide, she was almost panting in expectation.

'You remember, this Jesus you kept hearing about and then this Philip had promised to take you to see him?'

Freya nodded, but she was clutching her head, as if feeling again the terrible disappointment she had experienced when the Master, as Philip had called him, had seemingly refused.

Hermas continued. 'It seemed that their religious leaders had gone to Jesus demanding that he give them a sign to prove that he was their promised Messiah, and he said the only sign they would have was that of the prophet Jonah, who was three days and nights in the belly of the fish, and so it would be for him.'

Freya gave a little moan, as if she was afraid that she would never understand, or yet come to a satisfactory end to her story.

Hermas jumped up, anxious, and having given her water to drink, settled her on the couch and sat on the floor beside her as he continued.

'Freya,' he demanded her attention. 'Listen! This is why I have travelled at such haste to return to you, for this, *this* is the sign, the assurance we have all been seeking. This is why the story of Jonah is such an important part of our story.' Again he was quiet, while Freya had lifted herself so that she miss nothing.

'We had heard that they had crucified this man Jesus. Well, they buried him, for no one survives crucifixion, and for three days he lay there in the tomb, just as Jonah was in the belly of the fish, and then the next morning some women went to place spices in the tomb and ....'

Hermas turned then and taking Freya's two hands in his, assured her, 'the tomb was empty.'

'Had someone stolen his body?' Freya asked.

'No, no. How could they? The soldiers were guarding the tomb, and in any case, the grave clothes had been left, like a butterfly leaves its old cocoon.'

'Oh Hermas, can this indeed be true?' Freya was on her feet now in excitement.

'True, my Freya, yes true indeed. I have spoken to many who have seen and spoken with him. I longed to search until I found him for myself but I knew that I must return with all possible speed to share the news with my Beloved, that at last your broken heart might be healed.'

CHAPTER 23
GOOD NEWS INDEED

Freya slept peacefully that night in the arms of her husband, but when at last she woke he was already abroad and busy with the affairs of his estate. When he joined her on the veranda for breakfast she was ready with her questions, or - was it accusations?

'Oh Husband,' she reproached, 'I came so very close to meeting the Master before his terrible death, but now you hear that he is alive, and you were there, right in Jerusalem. Why did you not seek and seek until you too had met him?' She would have continued with her complaining, but he silenced her with a kiss.

'Hush, my dear one. Do not I long to meet him as much as you do? Can you not trust me? Now be patient, and I will tell you.

'I met many who had actually seen, yes, and even eaten with and touched the Lord. He stayed there in Jerusalem for forty days, but then, one day when he had gathered all the many who believed in him out on a mountain they call Olivet, suddenly they realised he was rising up above them, gradually at first, but then they were looking right up and he was disappearing into the clouds and at last they understood that he wouldn't be coming back for a while and he had left them to do his work.

'Once I heard that, I knew that I must come back home to you so that we could seek him together.'

Freya leaned back onto her couch, her eyes closed. Prisca had crept in on a mission, but Hermas, seeing her anxious glances, held his finger to his lips in assurance that there was no cause for concern. But as time passed, he sought to hold a flask to her lips, and then she struggled to sit upright. Pushing away the drink she began to speak.

'My Prince, oh how I thank the great God for bringing you back to me to share this great joy, but I am remembering how I had such a longing for you to return, and now I am understanding why. – Yes, yes, of course it is always painful to be parted from you for are we not made to be one? But something is happening, here too on our island kingdom, for some strangers have come with a message that seems to be changing lives and bringing great joy.

'Justus, the goat herd, has been piping wonderful songs of gladness, and has been promising to come and to tell me all about it, and yet he has not as yet come. I am glad now, because we will be able to listen together to his joyful message.'

Hermas rose. 'I'll see that nothing hinders his coming,' he declared, but then Freya, afraid she had raised his hopes in vain, became fearful.

'Oh, my husband, maybe I have raised our hopes foolishly. Oh, perhaps you should not go..' but Hermas was already gone.

It was two days later that Hermas, with his Freya leaning on his arm, made their way towards the village on the coast, and as they walked, others seemed to be joining with them so that a steady stream of people was making its way downward.

A shudder went through Freya. Hermas sought to wrap his own cloak around her. 'What is it, my Freya?' he questioned. 'Surely you are not cold?'

'There is a fear in my heart, for it was with such a crowd that we followed, all those years ago, and I was so sure that at last we were going to see this wonderful Jesus, but then – it was as if he refused to see us, - maybe because we were not Jews? I don't know. Then after that it was too late.'

Again she shuddered, and seemed to be in pain. 'Oh, I feel the pain now as if it were yesterday.'

Hermas turned back to where Maria was following and beckoned to her to take Freya's other arm, lest she collapse. It was then that Justus the goat herd skipped past them piping so happily on his pipe, it was as if he was leading them in glad assurance that some great joy awaited them.

The crowd was settling now, gathering quietly in expectation as a group of travellers seated themselves on the walls of their little fishing village. There was an older man who began by introducing themselves, and then went on to share the wonderful news of this Jewish Rabbi, Jesus. He shared their own bitter disappointment as this one whom they had believed to be sent from God, the one who would save them from the oppression of Rome, had been crucified and buried in the tomb. –

It was when he likened his death to the experience of the prophet Jonah who, wrapped in seaweed, had been incarcerated in the stomach of the great fish, and then had been vomited up alive, that Hermas and Freya gazed at each other in amazement. Hermas, of course, was remembering his strange dream, or was it vision, when in the storm on the Great Sea, but for Freya there was another memory that had been awakened.

She knew what it was now, this scent, or rather odour that seemed rooted deeply in her nasal passages often times as she wakened from sleep. Of course, now she recognised it. Yes, it was of seaweed. The old Spice Traders had told her of the seaweed which, having wrapped itself around her as a little baby, had kept her so miraculously from drowning.

But it was the young woman now beginning to speak who caught Freya's attention again. She was talking about her father, one Philip, who had wanted so much to come on this trip, to share the good news of their wonderful Messiah who was alive, having been raised up from the dead. It was he, Philip, who had wanted them to bring this wonderful story to the people living on these islands.

Her father had told her the story of these Spice Traders, and of one young woman in particular, who had so much wanted to meet this Jesus, and how grieved he had been that he had had to send them away disappointed.

Hermas turned and gazed at his wife in wide-eyed wonder, whereas his Freya seemed to be clinging to her seat as if she felt she might be ejected upward.

Another of the young men was continuing with his own account, but when at last the group were dispersing among the crowd, clusters gathering around them, Hermas left Freya with her faithful friends, hoping to contact the young woman who had said she was the daughter of Philip, one of the disciples.

He came back with the assurance that she would come with some of her companions to visit them on their own estate on the next morning, for the daylight was already fading.

Freya was so disappointed, but her husband reassured her. 'Morning will come, my Spice Maiden, and you will not be disappointed. I have a feeling that there is a higher power at work on your behalf. A new day is dawning for us all, of that I am sure.

'It was not by chance that we have been brought together. Somehow I believe we are part of a much greater story.

'We will return to our nest, even as the birds do, and you'll see. Tomorrow we will have our eyes opened to see and hear even more wonderful things.'

Oh, might it indeed be so? Freya was convinced that she would not sleep that night because of the hopes and fears that were tumbling in her mind.

CHAPTER 24
GOOD NEWS OF GREAT JOY

In spite of her fears Freya had slept soundly but was awake before dawn had broken, and dressed and breakfasted before their watchman, the goat herd, had piped his first notes to tell them the party from the coast was on its way.

Even as she had run down the path to welcome her dear Maria when she first came to the island, so now, ahead of the rest of the appointed delegation, she ran on until the strangers appeared over a rise.

But her husband had overtaken Freya, cautioning her to slow down.

'Our guests will need rest and refreshing before you begin to ply them with questions. I know – you have waited so long – and now you are hoping to have all your questions answered. I know, I know, but we must treat our guests graciously.'

And so the little party gathered in a shady bower, where the fragrance of the pomegranate trees wafted over them. At last, all fed and watered, a young woman among the party asked to speak. A faint bleating from the hillsides and the occasional twittering from the swallows was the only sound to be heard. Even the little prince and his friends sat, snuggled near to their mothers, in expectation too.

'Although my grandfather came from Greece,' she began, 'we were brought up in Galilee. My father joined in the fishing industry and it was there that he met up with this young prophet, Jesus of Nazareth.

'For many moons we rarely saw our father, for it seemed he had become obsessed with this Jesus. He sent us a message to say he was called to be one of his followers.

'Since he has returned to us he had told us so many wonderful stories of this Jesus; of his miracles and his teachings. 'Oh, Abba' we have said, 'If only we had seen him too. Why did you not send for us to come so we could have been there with him? And now it is too late.'

Oh, how Freya identified with her sad words. 'Oh yes, sad, sad.' Her eyes were full of tears, but the young woman was beside her, seeking to dry her eyes.

'No, no!' She assured her. 'You see, the chief priests and important men would not believe that this Jesus had come from God and so they plotted for him to be killed.'

Some of the older men in their group were not willing for this daughter of Philip, to be doing all the talking. One and another butted in to tell how this Jesus had been so horribly killed, how, indisputably he was dead and they buried him, but somehow his body was not in the tomb where he had been buried, and then, eventually how he had appeared to one and another until in the end they all knew without any doubt he had risen from death.

Here the young woman respectfully begged their permission to add this story.

'My Abba, Philip, told me this story so that I should not be sad that I had not seen Jesus for myself.

'Jesus had appeared to his disciples as they were gathered together in this upper room, but somehow Thomas, one of his followers, was never there, and he refused to believe their accounts. He told them, 'Unless I see him for myself, and can put my finger into the wounds where they nailed him to the cross, I will not believe that it really is the Master,' and then, suddenly, it was Jesus, standing there. He had heard every word Thomas had said, and he called him to come and put his finger in his hand, where those terrible wounds still showed.

'Poor Thomas! He was so ashamed, but so happy too, but Jesus told him, 'Yes, Thomas, you believe now because you have seen me, but there are many others who will never ever see me and yet they will believe in me. These will be among the happiest people of all.'

'So you see, I am one of those happiest of all people, and you, My Lady, you can be too.' Standing beside Freya, she gently placed her hand on her shoulder.

They continued with their stories, yes even through the heat of the day, for they had so much more to tell, and it seemed the folk from this island kingdom had always more to ask.

They were up early again the next morning to gather once more with their visitors, this time at the harbour side to await the ship which was coming to take them back to the mainland. But the young woman, Olivia, sought out Freya, and they sat together on a convenient rock.

'I wanted to tell you; there is a special reason why my Abba, Philip, wanted me to come with this party.' She went on then to recount the incident Freya remembered so well, and which had seemed to snuff out all the buoyancy and hopefulness of her youth and leave her struggling with doubts and fears.

'That is what my Abba told me. And this is why we have come here.

'You see, my father had met up with a group of Greeks, spice traders on their way to Jerusalem. It seems they had already heard rumours of Jesus, so when they knew that my father was a friend of his, they asked him how they could meet him. He assured them that he could help them, but felt awful because when they did meet up with him again he had to tell them that Jesus had not been willing, and of the strange words he had said, about a corn of wheat falling into the ground to die.

'Abba was so puzzled, because it did not seem like Jesus at all. And then, of course, everything seemed to go wrong and Jesus did, as it were, fall into the ground to die, though he could so easily have escaped from his enemies. Looking back he could see it was as if it was somehow meant.'

Olivia wrapped her arms around Freya, allowing her to weep a little, before she continued.

'It seemed an impossibility that we could meet up with you. After all, you might have continued your journeying as spice traders and been anywhere in the world, yet my father so prayed we should meet up with some of you and that you might know the end of the story -

'And of course it is the beginning too. Because now we know that Jesus did not just come for the people of Israel, but for everyone in the whole world. And he had not only come to preach to us, but to die in our place, so that God can forgive us all, so...................'

Olivia could not continue, for their ship was in dock and her friends were shouting to her to come aboard. Freya stood and waved until the ship's sails were just a speck on the horizon, and even when it was out of sight Hermas had to place his arm firmly around his wife and steer her homeward.

Freya seemed to be in a daze. It was as if she was unable to take in the wonderful message she had heard.

'Mama! Mama!' Her little son tried to demand her attention, and she would respond for a few moments, to share with him his joy in some flower that had opened up its beauty, but her interest was short lived.

Hermas however was like the goatherd. Somehow he had been able to grasp straight away the implications of the message that had been brought to them.

This Jesus he had been seeking was alive. He had come out of the tomb even as Jonah could not be kept in the belly of that great fish.

Freya did not seem to be concerned as to her husband's whereabouts, so, once home, he was off into the hills. A great joy was welling up inside him, and he found he was uttering words of praise and joy that had never been in his vocabulary until that day, and then, wonderfully, mystically it seemed, he found he was in conversation, and he knew that this wonderful Saviour he had so longed to meet, was walking beside him, speaking into his heart and life.

He wanted to rush home that his Freya might truly understand and share his experience, but it was as if a hand was reached out to check him. 'Wait, my Son. No need to rush. Wait and rest and see what I will do.'

But he so wanted to run to her. Waiting was much harder. He reasoned with himself that it was his duty to go to Freya. He began to walk toward the homestead, but his feet grew heavy and the joy seeping from his heart.

CHAPTER 25
GOOD NEWS TO SHARE

Freya had slept through the heat of the day. Waking she splashed water into her face and wandered aimlessly into the garden. It was as if too much information had been piled into her mind and she could not take it all in.

She found herself near to the garden beds where Maria had first come upon her. She had been struggling then with the project her husband had planned for her, to cultivate some perfume that might bring joy to many – was he merely seeking riches was the question that kept on rising. She had had no heart for this project, and though deep down she had known her husband was only concerned for her good, somehow she had struggled to work with him.

But now there was the possibility of a joy that had no need of riches or possessions to enhance it. Olivia and her friends had this joy; and now Justus, the goat herd. Yes, for undoubtedly he too was changed since he had met with these people from Galilee. And what of the Prince Hermas? Something was happening to him. Was it possible that this Jesus who had impacted her life throughout her journeying, was actually here with them? She had become aware of the wonderful fragrance of his presence as the story of his life had opened up to her, preparing her so that it seemed that to meet with this Wonderful One was all that could satisfy her. So could it be true, that this wonderful one, this Jesus, was actually now here with them?

Words from the beautiful love story her husband had sent to her began to infiltrate into her mind. Quietly she began to sing;

>'Rise up, my love, my dove, and come away
>
>Winter is past, your prison house of pain
>
>Is broken and I'm come to make you whole again
>
>Rise up my love, my dove and come away.'

She rose from the bench where she had been sitting and began to dance, gently at first, her steps slow and cautious, but as if the beat of some far off music was quickening its pace, she began to dance with glad abandon, until at last, exhausted, she flung herself on a grassy bank and wept great tears of healing and of joy.

>'Thank you, Lord Jesus, thank you,' she murmured.

'Mama, my Mama. ' Her little Pilipos flung himself into her arms. Smothering him with kisses she so wanted to introduce him to this Wonderful One, the source of all fragrance and of joy, who had not only conquered death, who had proved himself to be alive in so many wonderful ways: and yes, had drawn near so that she knew, not only that he was alive, but that he was here with her, in her heart and life.

Rising, she began to lead her little son as they sang one of the songs that the Galileans had taught them:

> 'Jesus, Jesus, only Saviour
>
> Only way to heaven above
>
> Jesus, Jesus, dying for us
>
> Come to show the Father's love.'

The circle was ever widening as the prince's playmates and their carers were all joining in. Yes, dear Maria, and Prisca too seemed to be renewed so that even their increasingly feeble limbs enabled them to join in the jubilation.

The sun had crept high above them and they needed to seek the shade. As they walked back to the house, Freya noted that Hermas was deep in conversation with Justus, the goat herd, who somehow had managed to join the company, but it wasn't until they had all eaten and then rested that he shared the matter with his wife.

'You know, my Freya, we have a great responsibility now to share this wonderful news. I think you have been seeking this, our Lord Jesus, all your life, whereas I had been content to seek a beautiful wife, -(here of course, his speech was interrupted with a lingering kiss) But of course it was through the gift that you were to me that I became involved in your search for the Saviour. Oh what a wonderful joy we are now sharing.'

'Yes, we do have to share it, don't we?'

'That is what I was talking to Justus about.'

So it was that there was the beginnings of a church there in their island kingdom of Fairwinds.

Freya would often teach them songs, yes, and sometimes dances too, that were based on as much of God's word as was available to them. Sometimes excerpts had been hand copied and eventually reached to them from the mainland. A time would come when wonderful letters from Paul, a Jewish teacher and now a follower of Jesus, - Christians as they were now called, were passed on to them.

Freya was always busy in her garden, while Hermas sometimes travelled and would bring back new spices and fragrances. Together they would extract and distil while people came from near and then further afield as word spread of her ministry of healing.

Prince Pilipas was proving a good scholar and would often read aloud when they gathered together for a church gathering. With the ideal climate and sheltered existence, it seemed to Freya that nothing could ever drag her from her island kingdom.

When Hermas called her to join her on a walk up to see the new born lambs Freya had no thought of any impending change or that her secure kingdom was about to be shaken.

'You know, my love, that once we have refined this very special fragrance that we will not be able to keep it to ourselves. Men will come from far and near to purchase it and take it back to their wives.'

Freya let go of his hand and turned to face him. No, she certainly had not thought of that possibility. But Hermas was continuing.

'But Freya, in not only learning that Jesus of Nazareth is alive but that he is here with us, in our hearts and lives, we are in possession of a message that is of far greater worth than the most wonderful perfume.

'Freya, we can't keep it to ourselves. Yes. Of course this news is not for sale. But just as Philip's daughter felt this urge to take this dangerous journey across the straights so that we might become Christians, we have got to share this good news with others.'

Freya had turned aside to find a convenient log they could sit on for she felt her legs going weak.

'What are you thinking of?' Her words came out as a gasp.

Hermas turned and half rose so that he could grasp both her hands before he answered her.

'What about your grandparents?' he asked. 'I took great risk and faced many dangers in order that I might find out for you your roots.'

Freya saw where this was going and pulled away from her husband.

'We sent a messenger to tell them of the birth of our son.' She was speaking defensively.

'But we don't know that they ever got the message. And now we have a far greater message, a message of God's own son.'

Freya turned and snuggled beside Hermas there as the evening sun was sinking below the horizon. She brought no more arguments, but inside her a war was raging.

CHAPTER 26
FRESH CHALLENGES

Freya awoke from a troubled sleep. Her husband had left her at the first crack of dawn and was already busy on their estate, and it was her dear Maria who came in to help her to face the new day.

She coaxed her to allow her to bathe her face and drink the mixture of fruit juices she had prepared, and now at last Freya had slipped into a robe and had come to sit with her on the veranda, ready, she hoped, to talk.

'Oh Maria. I was dreaming about the ship again last night. I thought that nightmare had ended, but…but…'

Maria's heart ached for her. Was there no healing that could restore to her the feisty little Spice Maiden who had secured a place in her heart all those years ago?

She moved one of the screens so that they might have privacy as she drew the girl near to allow her to weep on her shoulder. How many bottles had her tears yet to fill?

'Now, my lamb. Tell your Nona what it is that is troubling you,' and between sobs and snuffles Freya poured out her fear of setting out on this dangerous journey, beyond the lands of Greece and Macedonia, across the isthmus on to the remote shores of Transylvania.

'But do *you* have to go?' Maria questioned. 'Surely your husband could take some of the others with him?'

Silently, spite of tears streaming again from her now bloodshot eyes, Freya shook her head. There was nothing Maria could do but wait for more.

At last she continued. 'No Maria. I guess I am going through what my own mother must have gone through when she accompanied my father while I was so little, for I believe God wants us to go as a family, somehow to make up to my grandparents what they have suffered.'

Maria knew she must say no more. Instead she held her Spice Maiden the closer and wept with her. When eventually dear Prisca came to see if they were ready for food they shared with her and together they knelt in prayer, asking the God of all comfort to deliver them from all their fears and that he would be their confidence and joy as they set out together on this yet another perilous journey, for the older women were determined that they too would not be left behind.

CHAPTER 27
A CORN OF WHEAT BRINGING FORTH MUCH FRUIT

Maria and Prisca, too old now to join in the household chores, sat in a sheltered arbour watching the steady stream of people who walked up from the shore, or across the hills, to come to Freya's house of healing.

Yes, the Prince Hermas had realised that, if they were to have any privacy at all, that his wife needed a separate building where she could store all her herbs and medicines, and meet with the many needy people who came, not just with the ailments of their bodies, but with all the pain that they carried in their hearts.

'What a blessing that she took courage to go with the Prince to visit her own people,' Maria murmured to her dear friend.

Prisca did not hurry to reply. They remembered what a dangerous crossing it had been, when Freya, for the first time, entered into something of the trauma her own mother must have endured when, a young woman like herself, and in a far more terrible gale, her child had been snatched from her arms.

'She was mostly terrified for the little prince,' they remembered.

They watched awhile as, a little one no longer, the Prince Pilipos himself appeared. He had maintained his love of the herbs and fragrances and was kept busy in the distillery where he had trained some of his companions to work with him. But that was not his main calling in life, for he was one of the keenest of the little band of Christians who met now, not only down by the harbour, but throughout the villages of their island. They would travel in twos and threes to visit the various groups to teach them from the letters that were sent to them from some of Jesus' own disciples. They were even planning to travel further afield.

The sun was at its zenith, and the two older women now rose in their role as her faithful guardians, and insisted that Freya leave her ministries and come to the house for rest and refreshment, while others explained that she would be there again the next morning.

It was later in the day that her two faithful mothers had an opportunity to join Freya as she sat contentedly on the balcony, waiting for her husband to return for their evening meal.

'We were talking this morning about how different your life had been since you made that journey to visit your people,' Prisca began, hesitantly, but Freya was eager to talk.

'Oh, but someone had set out on an equally hazardous journey before that....'

The older women pricked up their ears, surprised.

'Yes, indeed. Remember those people who came from the land of Judah? Christians, yes. Philip's daughter was among them?'

'Yes, yes.' Prisca joined the story. 'It was they who first told us the wonderful news that though Jesus had died, that he didn't stay in the grave. That he is alive.'

'Yes,' said Freya. 'And they not only told us that he is alive, but best of all, they brought Jesus with them. And though they could not stay with us, they taught us that we can ask Jesus to stay with us and to live in our hearts, and – and-'

As Freya was speaking, she was alive with the joy of God glowing and shining from her whole being.

'Yes, and he is, isn't he?' Maria affirmed. 'It was that that gave you courage to set out on that, your last dangerous journey.'

Freya sat, quiet awhile, realising perhaps for the first time how wonderfully her life had been changed since she had learned, not only that this Jesus, the one she had been seeking all her life, had indeed died, but he had conquered death, broken out of the tomb where he was buried, and was alive indeed. But he was no longer here on this earth as a man as he had been.

Philip's daughter had sought her out before they were leaving and had taught her to pray to this Holy One and ask him to come into her heart and life. But it was after they had gone and they had agreed to meet regularly with the little group of Christians from the goat herd's village that she learned the wonderful teaching that all her sins could be forgiven.

And then this nagging persistence that she needed to make this dangerous journey to visit her grandparents? Could this be his voice? The voice she had never come to hear on earth? Only as she agreed with the Prince that they must go as a family did she have peace, and with this peace she became aware again of the fragrance, filling her days with joyful ministry.

It was Maria who broke the silence.

'You are carrying on the ministry of your mother, Freya,' she suggested gently.

'And not just of your mother.' It was the Prince Hermas who, having joined them, now stood with his hands resting on Freya's shoulders.

Freya turned her face, questioning.

'Why, you are carrying on the healing ministry of the Master, Jesus himself.'

There was stillness as they sat, enjoying the last rays of the evening sun. No words needed to be spoken, for each of them became aware of the beauty of the fragrance that was not only around, but within. Freya's fragrance maybe, but not only hers. It was a fragrance that they all knew they must carry abroad.

The End